W9-CFY-407

NORTHERN LITES

A FIRESIDE READING COMPANION

WRITTEN AND ILLUSTRATED BY
JACK KRAYWINKLE

ADVENTURE PUBLICATIONS, INC.
CAMBRIDGE, MINNESOTA

Dedication

This book is dedicated to my dear friend and sister, Nancy, for her editorial insight, faith, and constant encouragement.

In Appreciation

For my dear companion and loving wife, Kay, who encouraged me throughout the writing, and has been my steady promoter and a source of support.

Thanks

Thank you to those who first suggested I write down these stories; and to all who first heard them, and said yes.

Contents

Preface

Whether read aloud or in silence, Northern Lites is a collection of stories in the manner of those heard by a fire. The stories come from the threatened lonely land over Lake Superior, which is as harsh as it is fragile, unique in its character as well as in its history. Like the smoke from different kinds of wood, the stories are a blend of different flavors, each offering an impression of this very special land of rock, water and trees.

The Storyteller

A couple days out on a late season canoe trip a number of years ago, I arose early one morning to souring weather conditions. I decided to get some portages behind me before the weather deteriorated further. By midmorning the cold drizzle started, and I donned my fleece and rain suit, clamped my hat on my head and paddled grimly all day. By late afternoon, with rainwater soaking through seams and trickling down my neck and up my wrists, I began to doubt how much fun I was actually having. Still, I was determined to continue to my chosen destination, following my trip plan for the week.

I was traveling alone, something I really enjoy. Perhaps if I'd been traveling with someone we'd have stopped earlier when cold and fatigue set in. Probably for lack of anything better to do, I kept going. I prefer late fall trips to get away from other campers, and I had not encountered anyone since starting, but the dismal turn in the weather made me feel lonely. I'd just come to a big lake, and crossing it against a light but steady wind and rain, I began reconsidering the pleasures of traveling alone in the Boundary Waters wilderness.

Bone weary late in the day, I spotted a small point where I knew there was a good campsite on the lee side of an island, sheltered by tall pine and spruce. The thought of such an ideal refuge from the weather bolstered my morale. I used my fading energy to pull for the point.

As I drew nearer, my hopes of rest and refuge plummeted. Through my rain-spattered glasses I noted a haze of smoke hanging in the hollow of the pines around the campsite. Occupied. After not seeing anyone for three days, the thought of the one campsite I wanted being already taken disgusted me. Though drained of energy and chilled to the bone, the frustration gave me just enough warmth to paddle closer and investigate. Maybe I just felt it would be nice to talk to someone.

I was within a hundred yards when through the haze I could make out an overturned canoe on the shore, and someone standing beside it waving me in. For some reason, the need for companionship felt suddenly stronger. I paddled closer.

He stood in the steady drizzle on the sloping granite slab that sagged into the lake in front of the campsite. Beside him was his overturned, old wood and canvas canoe. He and the canoe looked like a well-matched set. He wore a heavy wool plaid shirt and a pair of baggy, dark, high-water pants held up by suspenders. His face was obscured by a broad-brimmed felt hat that drooped with the dripping rain water.

As I maneuvered my canoe broadside to the rock slab, he held the gunwale steady while I unfolded my stiff, aching limbs and stepped ashore. Then he gingerly helped haul my canoe up from the shore, all without a word. Without greeting he said he'd been watching me come across the lake and was expecting me. He asked if I'd care to share the campsite with him since it was late in the day and the weather so poor.

I looked out over the expanse of water I'd just crossed, and through the misty haze and fading daylight could not make out the shore I'd come from. He must have had amazing eyesight to have watched me cross that lake, I thought. I hadn't planned to share a campsite with anyone on this trip, but looking out over that cold, bleak lake with evening fast approaching, I said "thanks," I'd be pleased to join him, if it wouldn't be too inconvenient. I picked up my pack and followed him into the trees. It was darker under their shelter, but I smelled the piney smoke of his fire and detected the aroma of hot coffee mixed with it. The idea of sharing the site all at once seemed much better.

I looked for his tent, but all I could see was a big old canvas lean-to rigged close to the fire. The tarp fit right in. Either this guy was a die-hard traditionalist or couldn't afford new or better. He'd obviously been using this stuff for a long. No matter, it was shelter from the rain with a warm fire and hot coffee. I hauled my pack under his tarp and heaved a sigh as I crouched by his crackling fire. "Got a cup?" he asked.

I wasted no time digging my cup from my pack and he filled it with steaming coffee, strong and black. It was luxury to just hold the cup in my numb hands, but ecstasy to sip and let it warm me from the inside. I hadn't realized I was so chilled. We chatted about the weather outlook as the coffee warmed me. I pulled off my rain gear and tossed it onto my pack, and began to dry my clothing by the fire.

After stretching, I sat on a log he had pulled under the tarp so I could face the warmth of the fire, and he filled my cup again. While he did, I took in the contrast between us. I wore a modern nylon rain suit to stay dry; he wore wool. I wore polypropylene fleece for warmth; he wore wool. I carried a pack stuffed with the light-weight conveniences of today's technology; he had the barest of time-worn essentials. But somehow, as I ate a plate of his beans and drank his coffee in the early darkness that soggy evening, I felt remarkably warm and cozy under his weathered canvas tarp.

As warmth slowly seeped back into my body from the fire and nourishment, I assumed a more relaxed mood, like my new companion. I noted he was as completely at home under that tarp with the rain dripping all around us as I would be in my own living room. Lounging against my pack I let my aching muscles sag while studying the man a little more. He had tilted his hat back, revealing enough forehead to suggest he was bald, and what hair he had was gray. The grizzled whiskers hadn't seen a blade in a week or more. His skin was coarse and creased, probably wrinkled more from exposure to the elements than from age. His agility made me wonder how old he actually was. Bushy eyebrows hooded his squinty eyes so I couldn't determine their color, but when he looked at me the firelight flickered in them.

Apparently this fellow was a native of the area, and spent a lot of his time in these woods. As we sat together under the tarp, prodding the ends of burning sticks into the fire, I asked him about the area. A topic I never tire of hearing about.

Up until that point conversation had been stiff. He squatted by the fire and added another log. Then, taking a burning twig from the flames, he touched it to the stump of a pipe clamped in his mouth, and soon billows of tobacco smoke mingled with the sooty pinewood smog. His eyes glittered as he began to talk of the way things were here long ago; of old friends and obscure events. I was only half interested, until he began telling a story. Then I became an attentive listener. The thread of that story he skillfully wove into another, and then another, and yet another. He continued long into the night, as I made tea from my pack and he re-stoked his pipe. The rain quit but the soggy forest continued to drip, steeped with the rich scent of the wet earth in autumn. He talked on until I eventually fell asleep late in the night, my mind saturated with stories. The last thing I recall was the sound of his voice and the dripping trees, the smell of pine smoke and wet wool.

I awoke cold and shivering, still reclining against my pack. He had left. Sometime in the early hours he'd packed all his gear and moved on. The tarp, his canoe, there wasn't a trace that he'd even been there. I hadn't even learned his name. I looked across the fog-shrouded lake and neither saw nor heard anything. Damp and chilled, I stumbled around scrounging for wood to split for a fire to warm myself. As I sat in the smoke waiting for water to boil for my oatmeal, his stories started coming back to me.

And that's where these stories came from. I can't remember them all, but the gist of them is reconstructed here, though without the conditions or effects of his telling. I share them here for what they are — tales best told by a fire.

Kalamojakka

No one ever knew for sure why Sulo and Inga Makinen left their home in Finland to come to this country many years ago, but like many other immigrants, they missed their homeland. Undoubtedly, that was why they chose to settle in northeastern Minnesota, a region very similar to the land they had left behind. Sulo and Inga felt comfortable here. They soon found a beautiful site to make their new home. They settled in a remote area on a quiet little lake beside a noisy rushing stream.

As is common with Finnish people, they first built a sauna of cedar logs, using rocks from the lake for the firebox. Then they built their house of perfectly notched, solidly fitted pine logs, a small but cozy home. Sulo was a skilled craftsman with his ax, and he used it with other hand tools to make most of their furniture from trees.

Together they created a large garden patch, which was not easy because the shallow soil was poor. But they knew how to mulch and turn compost into soil, and Inga planted things she knew could thrive in harsh conditions. She was good at making things grow.

Sulo worked when he could as a wood cutter, or doing odd jobs for people around the area, but mostly their life was subsistence. Oh, they kept a cow or a goat periodically, and always had a few chickens around, but would never be considered farmers by anyone who knew farming.

They didn't have much, and never wanted much, but they got by. What they did have in abundance was a deep love for each other. It wasn't a love expressed in words; there wasn't a need for that. It showed when they took each other's hands, or in their eyes when they looked at each other at the end of a day and understood. Together they were a team that pulled in the same yoke, each sensing what was needed and responding without words.

So this was their life of quiet companionship deep in the woods, and both Sulo and Inga loved the land as they loved each other. They had no children, but wild creatures were frequent visitors, and they cared for them and shared with them, especially the birds.

Sulo bargained with a farmer every year for grain and corn to feed the birds, and chickadees often perched on Inga's head as she filled their feeder. When she worked on her hands and knees pulling weeds in the garden, the birds worked beside her pulling worms. Sulo enjoyed listening to Inga mimic the calls of birds as they tended the garden, or singing in her sweet, clear voice the old Finnish folk songs he loved so well.

The stream beside their cabin tumbled over and around dark granite bedrock before joining the lake, where its flow at the mouth kept the water open well into early winter until the cold claimed it. Migrating ducks and geese stopped there, and Sulo took corn to them, soon gaining their trust. Sometimes he'd hold one in his arms and gently melt ice from its beak with the warmth of his bare hands. One fall a goose showed up dragging a wing which was broken beyond healing, hanging on only by connecting skin. For several days Sulo watched as the goose ate the corn, and he realized it wouldn't survive in that condition. Luring the big bird close with a handful of corn, he entrapped it in his strong arms and deftly severed the dangling wing with his puukko (knife), so the stump could heal. The goose seemed to understand, and stayed with Sulo and Inga for a long time.

Sulo enjoyed fishing. Sometimes Inga fished too, but Sulo was always eager to fish, and he went year round. In the summer, the two of them fished from a little boat he'd built, but in the winter he fished alone through the ice.

Inga preferred to stay at home where it was warm, and knit mittens for Sulo.

They ate fish prepared just about every way possible, boiled fish, baked fish, fried fish, smoked fish or dried fish — fish of any kind. The lake always provided, and though they could always count on fish, they couldn't always count on how many. When their appetites were big but the fish were small or few, Inga used an old Finish recipe to make "kalamojakka," a fish soup or stew made from, well... pretty much everything that makes a fish.

Over the years, Sulo and Inga aged with the land. Their blond hair turned white as snow, and Inga's eyes – once sky blue – now showed clouds as her vision began to fail. She liked to knit, but now needed daylight to do it. Together they could still do all the chores; it just took a little longer. Though Sulo was still strong, there had been spells over the past year that told him it might be his heart.

The first spell he attributed to "summer heat," and he went home and rested. Later, other spells warned that it was more than the weather. Sulo was not concerned for himself; he was at peace with being part of the natural cycle of things. His concern was for Inga. He hadn't told her about his spells, afraid she would want to move away because of concern for him, perhaps to a town where there were doctors. Sulo couldn't bear the thought of leaving their homestead. Now as they worked together, he was often silent. How could he help her if his heart stopped? Could she manage without him? He thought about how to tell Inga of his spells and what he could do to prepare her.

Inga knew there was something on Sulo's mind, so when Sulo told her he was going fishing early one midwinter day, she felt it would be good for him to be alone for awhile. She knew he would share his thoughts with her when the time was right. Sulo told her he would take the pulk sled and ski across the black spruce and tamarack swamp on the south end of their lake, to a much bigger lake. There, he told her, the fish might be bigger and maybe his luck would be better.

It didn't take him long to prepare, and after a final cup of coffee he kissed Inga on the cheek and told her he probably wouldn't be back until after the sun had set. After fastening the harness belt of the pulk sled, Sulo strapped on his skis. As he set off, soft pre-dawn light stretched long, dark silhouettes of trees over the snow.

Sweet popple smoke from their cabin scented the air, but that was soon left behind. The winter air was utterly pure. Distilled by the cold, it held no scent or flavor. Each breath Sulo drew pinched his nostrils, and when exhaled it hung in the air as a brief cloud until the cold reclaimed it. In the fragile, frozen silence, it seemed as though the crystal atmosphere could support no more sound than the simple hissing of his skis over the satin snow.

Exhilarated by the bracing cold, Sulo felt he was flying along. He loved to ski, and this was skiing at its best. It didn't take him long to reach the south shore of the lake, and the stars were fading in the brightening blue sky as he started into the dark swamp of spruce and tamarack. Completely familiar with the land, he soon found a suitable route through the tag alder along a frozen beaver channel that led deep into a swamp where it joined a stream. Winding through the trees, he followed it toward the big lake.

In the swamp Sulo took time to watch for signs of activity. He steered clear of open water where beaver had been operating, and telltale signs of thin ice. While skiing past a deep drift, Sulo was startled by a grouse which exploded from under the snow beside him in a flurry of fluttering wings. He knew the signs of every creature that lived there, and could tell what they had been up to by looking at their tracks in the snow. Their distraction caused Sulo to take over an hour to get through the swamp, but eventually he reached the big lake.

Once on the open ice, he was flying again. The sun was just over the treetops and Sulo made long strides down the main part of the big lake to a bay where luck had always been good. When he got to the bay, he checked landmarks on the shore and picked a likely spot. In no time Sulo had his skis off, cleared away a patch of snow and put the ice chisel to work. After making a hole through over three feet of ice, he scooped out the slush, pulled up his sled beside the hole and prepared his tackle. Finally, seating himself on the sled box, he set to the business he'd come for.

Overhead the sky was a deep, clear blue, and though the sun still rode low, days were growing longer again. Though the land was still in the firm grasp of winter, Sulo could feel the sun warm his back as he jigged the bait. He took out the leftover pancakes that Inga had stuffed into his pocket when he left, and slowly ate them as he stared at the hole in the ice. Before long a trembling pull on the line told him the trip was not in vain. Hand-over-hand he retrieved the line, and brought up a nice pike over two hand-spans in length. For Sulo this was about as perfect as things could get. He put his lure back into the water and before long pulled in a nice crappie, then another pike, and yet another. There would be plenty of fish for both him and Inga to eat their fill, no need to make kalamojakka. In fact, the fish were biting so often, he forgot about his spells and figuring out how he would tell Inga about the problem with his heart.

He was catching so many fish he didn't notice the clouds moving swiftly down from the northwest. Just after midday the fish quit biting, and random flakes of snow tentatively made their way to earth. Sulo noticed a chill as heavy clouds moved across the sun. With the chill he seemed to sense an uneasy presence, and the feeling he was being watched.

Ridiculous, he thought; he couldn't be more alone. Still, he looked up and scanned the distant shore. There was no one. He kept jigging the bait, but the feeling of being watched wouldn't go away. He tried to think of what to tell Inga about his heart, but the uneasiness was so strong Sulo couldn't concentrate. He turned to look back over his shoulder.

There, about ten feet behind Sulo, crouched a huge, gray timber wolf on its haunches, its wild, hungry eyes seeming to stare into his soul. An icy gust of northwest wind stroked Sulo's cheek, but it was the wolf's stare that sent shivers running through him. As they looked at each other, Sulo's memory flashed pictures of ravaged deer carcasses he'd found over the years, and he nervously looked around for signs of a pack.

The wolf, a female, had materialized from nowhere. How had he not noticed her approach? Was she part of a pack? Maybe she would eat fish instead of him, he reasoned. Slowly he reached for the last fish he'd caught, and tossed it to the big wolf. After a couple sniffs, she devoured the fish in two gulps. Sulo tossed another fish, and then another, each one disappearing as quickly as the last.

"These fish were for me and my Inga," he complained, but the wolf continued to eat until nearly half Sulo's catch was gone. With the wolf well fed, Sulo felt a bit less vulnerable, but now the snow was coming harder, carried on an aggressive wind.

Only after the wolf's hunger seemed satisfied did Sulo notice the developing weather situation — as if the wolf had awakened him from a spell cast by the good fishing. In what seemed only moments, the snow had begun falling heavily, and now the wind had become the predator.

Sulo looked north across the vast expanse of ice he had crossed that morning and saw only a curtain of white. The tracks of his skis were drifting over. Quickly, Sulo gathered his fishing gear and what was left of his catch, keeping one eye on the wolf. She had not left after eating the fish, but sat watching from a distance. He harnessed himself to the pulk and strapped on his skis. Looking back at the wolf, Sulo said grudgingly, "you're welcome for the fish," then headed into the wind, toward home.

He had thoughts of the wolf running him down like a deer, selecting the weak and old by instinct. Encumbered by skis and sled, it would be impossible to fight off an attack. He forced the thought from his mind. Each blast of wind and stinging snow told Sulo he had to get off that lake soon, back home to Inga, back home to safety. Safe from the storm and the wolf.

For awhile Sulo followed his fading ski tracks from that morning, but in a short time they were wiped out. He had not taken his compass because he knew the area well and found his way by landmarks. Familiarity with the land was all he'd ever needed, but now there were no landmarks... only white. An hour before he had been fishing in the vast outdoors; now the whiteout created a claustrophobic feeling, as he realized that he no longer knew what direction he was traveling. He continued, lost in the blinding snow and vicious wind. Though he couldn't see, he knew that just beyond the white curtain a wolf was watching him.

Sulo could feel the wind's power blowing away his warmth and energy. He was tired, feeling his age, but thoughts of Inga kept him going. He thought about his heart. This would be a bad time for a spell. When he looked up, the wind took his breath away. He wanted to lie down and rest, but knew he'd never get up. If this was to be his end, he was ready to accept it. But what was to become of Inga? He had to get off that lake. If he could just get to the shoreline and find shelter in the trees, he'd build a fire. But there was only the white wind.

He tried to concentrate on keeping his skis going in a straight line with his head down to avoid the wind as best he could. Looking down he eventually noticed marks in the snow. It took awhile before he realized he was seeing something other than white. He stopped and knelt beside the marks. They were tracks. Fresh wolf tracks.

It dawned on Sulo that the wolf didn't want to be out on the lake in the storm either, and its sense of smell and instinct could guide it to the shore. With nothing to lose, Sulo decided to follow those tracks. If only the wolf wouldn't get too far ahead so the snow would drift over them. At times, Sulo could make out the ghostly, veiled form of the wolf just ahead of him. Sometimes it paused to look back at Sulo as though offering encouragement, or making sure he was still following.

He didn't know how long they traveled that way, but finally Sulo could hear the wind in the tops of the tall pines before he could see them. Just in time too, because the white curtain was turning gray as daylight faded.

When he reached the shoreline, Sulo made his way inland just far enough to find shelter in a thick stand of spruce and balsam. It was a relief just to be out of the freezing wind. He unhitched himself from the pulk, took off his skis, and got his ax from the box. First things first, and first was a fire.

In a short time he gathered a supply of dry pine from a nearby deadfall and kicked away a circle of snow among the thick evergreens. He touched a match to the twigs, and soon the fire provided warmth as well as light. Next, Sulo fashioned a lean-to frame close to the fire. He cut boughs to cover the frame, and made a thick mat of boughs to lay on. As he built his shelter in the snow, he was glad Inga was safe in the warm home they had built together. He hoped she wouldn't worry too much for him.

After gathering more firewood, he brought the little sled beside the shelter to see what else he could use. There was a ragged old wool blanket and the bucket of fish he'd caught, but not much else. He dug through his pockets where the cold pancakes had been, but found only an old tea bag from an earlier outing. Not much, but it might be enough.

It was dark now, but not so cold in his shelter by the fire. The night would not be pleasant, but for the first time since he'd caught the last fish, Sulo had a positive outlook. He didn't know exactly where he was, but for now that didn't matter. He was hungry. All he'd had since breakfast were the few cold pancakes Inga had put in his pocket. He set the frozen fish inside the lean-to, filled the bucket with snow and set it on the fire to melt for tea water. While cleaning a fish, Sulo sensed a movement at the dim edge of the firelight, and he peered through the smoke at a pair of glowing wild eyes.

"Ah, you're still with me," Sulo said aloud to the wolf, "and you've come to dinner again. At least you haven't come to eat me," Sulo said, only half sure, as he glanced around for others. The wolf, or her pack – if there was one – could have taken him any time. Was it a loner? Unusual. Where was the pack? Sulo reached for a large frozen fish and tossed it to the wolf, who picked it up and retreated into the shadows. Perhaps a well-fed wolf is not a threat, he reasoned, and besides it should have a reward for leading him to the safety of the trees.

He put the steaked fish on a spit to roast over the fire, then ventured out to a nearby birch tree. After peeling some bark strips, he returned to his shelter and fashioned a cone-shaped cup. By the time he'd eaten the fish, the water was hot, and Sulo made tea in his birch bark cup. He was thirsty, and the hot brew warmed him inside. He drank tea until the bag would no longer make tea.

As he sipped the hot tea and gazed into the fire, the snow continued to fall heavily and the wind roared in the tall pines over his head. He thought about what it would be like out on the lake right then, and Sulo knew he'd probably be dead by now. Instead, he was safe in his shelter, reasonably warm and dry by the fire, thanks to… a wolf, a wild wolf.

This was going to be something to tell Inga. His thoughts returned to his dear Inga, how she must be worrying for him in the storm. She must be worried for him right now, and he felt sorry for that. Concern for her had brought him out on this fishing trip in the first place – to find a way to tell her about his poor heart. How would he do it? Would she be able to carry on without him if he died? Who would take care of her, be her companion? They were such a team. Would she be able to continue? A shadowy movement to the side of Sulo's shelter caught his attention. The wolf was back.

Too exhausted to worry about the wolf, Sulo put a couple big pieces of wood on the fire, pulled the old wool blanket around him and tried to get comfortable against the sled. Why did the wolf stay around? Why had it come so close in the first place? Sulo was too tired to think. Pulling his parka hood over his face, he tucked his hands into his armpits and curled up close to the fire in his little shelter. Soon he was asleep. As the storm sang its wind song, Sulo dreamed of Inga, and in his dream they reached out to each other, and touched.

He woke in the night, cold and shivering. The fire had burned down to coals, and he put on more wood and stoked the flames high again. Slowly warmth seeped back into him again, and in the fire's flickering light he thought he could see the wolf just off in the shadows. The storm was still blowing, but now the wind carried a different song – the singing of wolves. It was a sound Sulo had heard many times before, and it always gave him a tingle at the back of his neck. His four-legged companion heard it too, and he caught just a glimpse of the big wolf as it turned and loped off into the night. She's gone to join them, Sulo thought. In a sense, Sulo envied the wolf. He imagined it going off to be with its own kind, its own family. Maybe she had a mate. Just so she didn't bring them all back to him. Still tired, he hoped the fire would keep the pack away. After putting more wood on the flames, he resumed his position on the boughs and was soon in restless sleep, dreaming again of Inga.

He slept long this time, and when he woke Sulo noticed it was getting light. His front side, which faced the fire, was cold. The fire had gone out. His back and the rest of him seemed strangely warm. He lay awhile half awake, until consciousness crept in. Where was the warmth coming from? He felt something behind him and stirred his stiff, cramped joints to roll just enough for a look. As he stirred, the big wolf arose from behind him and lunged out of the lean-to, almost knocking it apart as snow sifted through, covering Sulo. He was dumb-founded. The wolf had joined him in the shelter. He had intended to wake and feed the fire all night, but was so tired he hadn't. He might have frozen to death in his sleep, but the wolf had entered the lean-to and they had shared their warmth. Incredible. Would Inga ever believe it? Sulo wasn't sure he believed it. At least he knew there was no longer anything to fear from the wolf.

The wind was gusting lightly now, and only a light snow continued. Sulo gathered more wood in the dim morning light, and before long a blazing fire was crackling again. The bucket of snow went on the fire once more for hot water, but it wasn't until he started to clean another fish that he noticed the wolf was back. Again he tossed a fish to the wolf, but this time it was more out of friendship than a form of payment. Sulo spoke softly to the wolf, trying to gain her confidence. "You like my fish so much you decided not to go with the pack in the night," he said, but she kept her distance.

They were both hungry and ate a hearty breakfast of fish, and Sulo had many cups of hot fish broth while waiting for the weather to improve. As the daylight grew, it was apparent the storm had mostly passed. Now he could dimly make out the far shoreline, but watched for another hour as conditions slowly improved. It took awhile to get his bearings, but eventually he figured he had to backtrack to get to the swamp, back to his own small lake, and back home to Inga. In a little while, Sulo had gathered his things, hitched up his pulk harness, put on his skis and was ready to go again.

Over the lake ice, the new snow was hard-packed by the wind, and Sulo made good time. But in the woods and over the swamp the snow was soft and deep. The going was much slower than the day before and he had to stop often to rest, but made steady progress. He thought of Inga all the way, and he had so much to tell her. At last, by dusk he approached the shoreline in front of his cabin, a welcome sight. He could hardly wait.

When he got to the cabin, he called out to announce his return. After unhitching himself from the pulk, he took off his skis and stuck them upright in the snow outside the back door. She must not have seen or heard him approach. Delighted to be home, he again called out a joyful greeting. She was probably napping.

Sulo took his bucket of fish from the pulk. After all he'd been through, of all the fish he'd caught, there was only a small one left for the two of them. "Kalamojakka," he sighed.

Inga still had not come out to greet him. In the dim light of dusk he noted there were no birds at the empty feeder, no light inside the cabin, no smoke from the chimney.

Bursting through the back door of the cabin, he called out her name again. No reply. He could see the clouds of his breath as he stood there in the kitchen. No heat. To be cold enough to see his breath in the house, the fire must have been out since yesterday before the storm. After lighting a lamp, Sulo went to the sitting room to check the wood stove. There he found Inga in her rocker, cold and still beside the stove, a mitten she was knitting for him in her lap.

Outside in the distance, the wolf lifted her soft, sweet song to the stars in the evening sky.

The Drifting Canoe

It's always been tough to scratch out a living in the North Country, and the Great Depression didn't pull any punches when it hit the area in the 1930s. It offered a refuge for some who worked in C.C.C. camps, but any old timer who struggled through those years can tell you a thing or two about hardships. Some folks left in hopes of better prospects in more populous regions, but those who remained in the North Country in those days were real survivors. One thing that kept them from leaving was a genuine love of the land.

It wasn't that there was no work back then. Everything required work. The problem was finding a "work" that paid money to support a family. Just being able to work wasn't always enough to provide a living, where living could be enough of a challenge in itself.

Those times were hard on adults, and the future looked bleak for young people trying to make a start. But youthful spirits tend to trust more in fortune than faith. Fortune implies a risk, but if you've got nothing to loose, it makes sense to go for your dream.

The land of lakes and forests held a future in the heart of one certain young man. With his father he had learned to love the portage trails that linked the deep, clear lakes. Together they often traveled far into the wilderness in an old wood and canvas canoe.

The father and son painted the outside of the old vessel green every spring, and repaired and varnished the inside. It was weather-beaten and though patched many times, it still leaked. The old craft was heavy but floated light and free like the spirits of the man and boy it car-

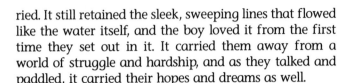

ried. It still retained the sleek, sweeping lines that flowed like the water itself, and the boy loved it from the first time they set out in it. It carried them away from a world of struggle and hardship, and as they talked and paddled, it carried their hopes and dreams as well.

The boy grew into his teens, and his father taught him how to fend for himself in the woods. They took longer trips, and as the young man grew in strength he learned to carry the canoe. On the water the three of them, the young man, his father and the canoe, traveled together. But it was on the portages that the canoe and young man first came to understand – and accept – each others' strengths and weaknesses. The result was an even deeper bond, and the young man learned to respect the canoe and felt as though somehow it had a spirit of its own.

But in the harsh reality of the depression world, the father had to take a job in a logging camp to make ends meet. That winter he was killed in an accident in the woods. The young man's mother was so distraught she left to live with relatives in Minneapolis. She explained to her son that he could come along or stay behind, but either way he was going to have to make his own way in the world. By his reason, if he was on his own he was where he wanted to be, and the young man opted to stay in the North Country.

Soon after his mother left, he became friends with an old man who was an outfitter in the little town. Over the next summer the old outfitter hired him to guide fishing parties. When the outfitter found how skilled the young man was, he even let him guide groups of important men from far away. His skill at being able to find the best places to fish gained him a good reputation as a guide. Perhaps it was luck, but to the young man it sometimes seemed that the canoe "knew" where to find fish, though he never shared that opinion with anyone. He also never seemed to get lost while traveling in his own canoe. On the rare occasion he was in a different canoe, however, he didn't seem to have the same kind of luck.

The outfitter and the young man shared their knowledge of the best fishing spots, and they mutually benefitted from working together in spite of the hard times. When they were drying or repairing gear they swapped stories of the woods and trip experiences.

When time permitted, the boy would hop into the canoe and go for a leisurely cruise down the shore of the lake on which the little town was situated. Sometimes hed grab his pack sack, which always held the few essentials he needed, and set out for a few days by himself in the vast border lake country.

During these trips, the old canoe and the young man became a part of each other. He was like a heart beating within the ribs of the canoe, and each stroke beat a strong, steady pulse. They became a denizen of lakes and streams while he paddled. On land, the old craft seemed to grow legs and spring over portage trails borne on the strong shoulders of the young man. Together, he and the canoe floated free of life's drudgery and the world was a beautiful place. There was no depression out on the canoe trails. Only dreams.

Being in the canoe made the young man feel close to his father, made all the dreams seem possible. But the warm summer days were growing shorter as well as cooler. With winter he knew the loneliness would be hard to bear without the canoe. He had been so busy over the summer he hadn't made many friends. Perhaps sensing the young man's loneliness that fall, the outfitter loaned him traps and showed him how to set them. A trap line would keep him busy and provide a small income over the long winter.

Freeze-up brought an end to the paddling season, and winter set in like another ice age. The young man fared well enough with trapping, but to him it was an unsatisfying business. The long, cold winter brought the inevitable loneliness, and the sight of the canoe covered with snow only deepened his depression. Sometimes he'd go brush the snow off the canoe, and run his hand along its hull. It seemed to retain the warmth of summer in its feel – or perhaps it was something only he could feel. But without being in the canoe, there seemed to be no opportunities to dream about the future, nor anyone to share the dreams. Eventually, he stopped dreaming altogether. Something was missing in his life.

Spring finally returned and the young man was busy again with the outfitter, preparing for another season. He anxiously worked on the canoe patching, painting, repairing and varnishing. Finally the ice went out and the young man was once again able to relieve his loneliness with evening excursions on the lake beside the little town.

But he didn't begin to dream again until he met a pretty young girl. She was with a few of her friends by the town dock one evening in early June. She seemed to stand out from the others as he paddled up to the dock after a short, lily-dipping tour in the waning sunlight. The girl asked about his canoe and he summoned the courage to ask her if she'd like to take a short ride. She said yes, taking her place in his heart from then on. Everyday he thought more and more about her and of being with her. The thoughts turned to dreams of the future, and the two of them together.

The pretty young girl's dreams became filled with the young man as well, and as the days and weeks went by they began seeing each other regularly. Neither had much money for dates, but he had the canoe. Evenings they'd often paddle around the moonlit lake, watching the lights of the little town fade behind them until they had to turn back. Sometimes they'd just drift, the three of them, and gaze up at the evening sky while sharing their dreams. They shared a love of the North Country, and much more. Both longed to make a place they could call their own. They dreamed of the things most young couples dream of, and being happy together forever. When apart they dreamed of each other, and when the young man's dreams drifted into the future, she was there with him.

Her family wasn't impressed with the young man. He had no money and they didn't believe he had much of a future. All her parents saw were the hard times of the depression. Besides, he was an immigrant's son, and a different nationality. It couldn't work. Her family never really took the young couple very seriously. Every time the young girl talked to her parents about the young man and their future, they pointed out all the difficulties of the depression, and how the young man could never amount to anything. She should consider leaving for a big city where hopes of getting a real job or finding a better man were more likely. But she knew she loved this independent young man who shared her dreams.

Together they began secretly planning for the future. They scrounged for cast-off household things, tools, any item they felt would be useful. They scraped and scrounged for money. He told her of a lake he knew to the northwest. It was a beautiful place in a bountiful area. That's where they'd go in his canoe. With no money, where else could they go? They'd tell no one. It wouldn't be easy, but it was the depression, and anywhere they'd go would be a struggle for them.

They let the old outfitter in on their plan, knowing he could be trusted. He liked the young couple and sympathized with them, perhaps because he too once had a dream. He donated some old packs and equipment, a map of the area, and hours of stories and advice that kept the couple laughing and excited about their venture. The outfitter offered to store their gear and hold what they couldn't take until they returned for it or gave up on their dream, which was probably what the old man expected. They kept their outfit in his shed at the water's edge near the town dock.

Finally, after weeks of scrounging and saving, they had the last item they'd be able to take, at least for now – a small, cast-iron cook stove. The young man disassembled it and bound it together so he could pack it on his back. They had their tools and items they'd need to build their cabin, and enough food to get them by for awhile.

Early the day of their planned departure, the old man helped them load the canoe with all the gear they could safely carry. He pushed them off as the first light was beginning to glow through the pines to the east. They set out in secrecy and moved swiftly across the glassy lake. The couple waved one last time to the old outfitter standing on the dock, then disappeared behind a point. They never returned for the rest of their gear.

Some weeks later, a fishing party the old man had outfitted, mentioned seeing an empty canoe adrift on a lake to the northwest. They didn't see anyone on the shoreline, and when they called out no one answered. They went after the canoe, but it seemed to drift elusively in the wind, keeping just beyond them, and they gave up. They said it looked like an old canoe anyway, wood and canvas type, green with patches... kind of weathered. Probably abandoned. The old man didn't think too much of it at first, but a second party that also happened to be in that area told of seeing the same green canoe.

After that, the old man started regularly directing fishing parties to the area. On their return, he made a point of casually asking them if they'd seen a young couple or their canoe. Sure enough, two other parties mentioned seeing a green canoe, apparently drifting empty. But no sign of a couple. The old man was puzzled and now a bit worried, but kept his concern to himself, faithfully preserving the couple's secret.

The girl's family, as well as the rest of the town, just figured the couple had eloped. But the old man knew the truth. He was haunted by questions and concern for the pair as winter approached with no sign or word from them.

Over the winter, the old outfitter inquired of trappers and loggers if they had seen any sign of a new cabin or the young couple. Nothing. If he were younger he'd have snowshoed to the area and searched, just to settle his fears. All he could do was wait out the snow.

Winter passed without any word or sign from the couple. In the spring the old man outfitted the first fishing party of the season. They returned after a successful trip, and before the outfitter could ask, they mentioned seeing an old, empty green canoe adrift on one of the lakes. Just thought it was odd, was all they said. The old man's hair stood up on his neck at the news.

Later that day he confessed to the family of the young girl what had happened the previous summer, and his fears. A search party went up to the area, but not a trace was found of the couple or their belongings. Family friends followed, looking for the young man and the pretty girl, but they never found a trace either. People started to doubt the old outfitter, preferring to believe the couple actually had eloped. But the old timer knew.

He remained faithful to their dream, and for years kept the rest of their gear waiting for them in his old shed down by the water. Summer evenings he often sat on the dock gazing across the lake, as if waiting for that canoe to round the point.

The couple has never been seen over all these years, never returned for the rest of their belongings. But the drifting canoe shows up every now and then to this day, floating empty on some lake in the canoe country. Some people say that if you catch the canoe, you will find it filled with all your dreams. All you have to do is get in and paddle it away. But if you do, like the young couple, you will never come back.

BuShag

BuShag was not her real name, it was a term she had been called long, long ago; and it stuck. She had long since forgotten its meaning as well as her real name. She was just BuShag.

No one among her people could remember when BuShag was not around. She had survived far more seasons than anyone else, and had outlived all other elders. BuShag in fact, could remember the births of those who were now called elders, and these elders claimed she had been old then. It seemed BuShag had always been old.

Her people measured time by the changing seasons, and as seasons continued to come and go, they blurred into a vague past. There was no telling how old BuShag was; no one had kept an account of her seasons. They had a word to describe her age, and it implied several things. In our language the closest translation might simply be "one who endures".

To look at her was to see time and earth personified. Shriveled and hunched over, she couldn't have stood much more than four feet tall. Her tiny head seemed to grow from a sunken chest. A deeply receding hairline left the front half of her head bare, and from that point a long, thick mane radiated like a pure white cloud. Her face was very dark, except for a pale yellow showing through where bone and skin came very close. Where the aged skin hung loose, it assumed an intricate pattern of deep creases which broke up her features like the imprint of a dark net. From under a heavy brow, yellowed eyes retained the flickering light reflected from countless fires. Her wrinkled nose sagged nearly flat over the deepest crease on her face, which sank into a toothless mouth. A tattered, dirty deerskin robe hung from her shrunken bony frame, and mukluks covered her bowed legs year-round. Her only adornment was a necklace of caribou teeth.

Most of the time BuShag stayed alone in her little hut, sitting on a pile of old caribou hides. Keeping irregular hours by night or day, she would alternate between sleep and meditation – puttering with some small animal bones, gathering roots and herbs for medicine, or preparing a broth or gruel, which was about all she could eat. Sometimes she sang strange songs or chants in a thin, crackly voice, like dry leaves rustling in the winter wind. Inside the hut, she moved about on all fours when she had to move at all. She seldom came out, but was quite capable of getting around at a slow lurching pace. She had a way of showing up unexpectedly anytime or anywhere in the village, which made a few people uncomfortable.

Among her people, age was revered. One survived in the north by wisdom as well as by luck. Wisdom was gained over the years, and success at survival in the harsh north could be attributed to accumulated wisdom. Since luck was beyond control, they believed it was granted by spirits. One who had luck was said to be favored by the spirits. Because of her great age, her people believed BuShag had tremendous wisdom, and was also on very good terms with the spirits. She had strong medicine.

As a medicine woman, BuShag was more than respected by her people; she was held in awe. Some even feared her, and invoked her name to add emphasis or add a dramatic effect in conversation. Perhaps they felt she was too close to the spirits. She had an uncanny way of reading signs and making accurate predictions. Not just predicting the weather by the way her joints ached, but predictions about people as well. Sometimes she could look at a child and tell what he or she would be good at as an adult. Sometimes she would tell a man something was going to happen, and it would.

One day BuShag told a man not to go fishing, because he might be killed by a fish. The man was a great fisherman and hunter, and bragged that he was not afraid of a fish, and that no fish could harm him. He was not afraid of old BuShag and her foolish ideas either. He went fishing, and came back with many fish, big ones. He bragged loudly of his skill, that he was not afraid of what BuShag said. He went to her hut and called to her, saying "foolish woman, see these fish I have caught. If I had done as you said and not gone fishing, we would not have all these fish to eat." That night, some of the fish were cooked to celebrate, and the man choked to death on a big fish bone.

There were other stories, told by the elders who had seen BuShag work her magic to heal sick people, or talk birds out of trees to come sit on her hand. Like her people, she knew the forest and the animals – when the time was right to hunt, and when to gather. But she also knew how to make medicine and talk with the spirits.

Sometimes she would tell her people stories that the elders of her own childhood had told. Stories about a people long ago that were like them, only different. She referred to these people as "the First Ones." BuShag's people referred to themselves as "The People." When she told the stories she often used words that were unfamiliar to The People. When she used those words, some believed her mind was gone and she was making up things to say. Even so, no one ever suggested the old medicine woman's stories might not be true. It would have been disrespectful.

Sometimes BuShag talked of strange creatures, animals that none of her people had ever seen. Fantastic animals in size and appearance, as well as in number. Then The People listened, not just because it was BuShag speaking, but because they had seen the pictures...

To them, it seemed the pictures had always been there; on rocks and cliffs above the water on many of the countless lakes. But many of the paintings, like the rocks themselves, were older than BuShag. No one knew who had painted them, not even the old medicine woman. Some pictures they could relate to, since they depicted hunters and canoes, with moose and other familiar animals. But other pictures showed strange creatures, and BuShag had to explain them and interpret their meaning. So when she told the stories she had heard so long ago, The People listened to her.

One day soon after the ice was gone from the lakes, a party of men from BuShag's people were away fishing. They had gathered many fish, and while they were drying them, some of the younger men decided to go look for caribou. They traveled far on the trail of some of the animals, and came to a distant lake. It wasn't a big lake, and the caribou had swum across it. Without their canoe, the men had to skirt around the shore and pick up the spoor of the deer on the other side. The caribou had come out of the water at a low spot next to a bare rock face which rose directly from the water at the shore line. When the hunters reached the place, a youth noticed strange marks on the rock, and stooped to investigate.

The marks were definitely more paintings, but this was a location none of his people had known of before. He called his uncle over to see them, and soon the group had forgotten the caribou and were studying the pictographs on the rock.

These were indeed strange markings, symbols none of them had ever seen on rock paintings before. Many markings and small animal signs, canoes full of men with holes for faces and other cryptic symbols. The paintings were laid out in a strange manner too, and overall just looked different from all the other rock pictures any of them had seen. They decided this was something to tell BuShag when they returned home.

Several days later the men returned and there was a celebration in the village to welcome them and the food they brought back. While the women cleaned and divided the fish, the youth who had discovered the paintings and his uncle took a nice fish from the catch and went to talk to BuShag about the rock pictures.

Because of her odd behavior and a reclusive attitude, BuShag's hut was set away from the others, in the trees at the edge of the village clearing. The discovery of the paintings was news the youth was entitled to bear to the old woman. The uncle went with him because BuShag probably would not hear the boy, and because both men were maybe just a bit afraid to visit the ancient medicine woman alone.

On reaching BuShag's hut, the two men sat themselves silently on the ground and waited quietly until she was ready to see them. They waited that way until after the sun had gone down. Finally BuShag pushed the door flap aside and peered at them. She muttered something not meant for them to hear and closed the door again. After a time she drew back the door again and sat in the opening.

The uncle offered BuShag the fish. The youth, who before had only seen her from a distance, winced a bit as her scrawny claw-like hand grasped and drew the fish inside the hut. They sat awhile longer in polite silence, contemplating each other's presence. Eventually the older man spoke, telling of the success of the fishing trip, the skills of the men and so on. Then after indicating to the youth to build up the embers between them into a fire, he was silent again.

BuShag conveyed the impression of being disturbed, and waited for them to go away and leave the fish. Noting her attitude, the uncle quickly mentioned the boy's discovery of more rock paintings. BuShag looked up from the fire into the man's eyes, and as he spoke he could sense her knowing more of the story than his words told. He described where the lake was, and the location of the rock paintings. Then he went into detail about the paintings themselves, giving such an accurate account of them that it impressed the boy, though he didn't dare show it.

Saving the best for last, the uncle began to describe the unusual, strange characters and symbols. He spoke as though he couldn't stop. As he spoke, the firelight revealed a change in the old medicine woman. Her intent stare into the storyteller's eyes became less fixed, until her own eyes fluttered and rolled back into her head, and then closed. Her head tilted back to one side leaving her mouth open. She seemed to be in a trance. As the story ended, she was crooning some eerie old song, which she stopped abruptly. Opening her eyes again she looked at the two men, who had become uneasy with her behavior, and told them to leave her alone. They didn't need to be told twice.

Several days passed, and each day the youth asked his uncle if BuShag knew something or had told him anything about the paintings yet, or was she just an old crazy woman. The uncle just shrugged his shoulders and kept mending his nets. One day, he stopped what he was doing and told the youth not to say she was crazy anymore.

Meanwhile, BuShag had stayed in her hut brooding over

42

the descriptions of the newly discovered paintings. She had always been fascinated by rock paintings, but none of the other paintings she had seen or heard of before had troubled her. For some reason, these were different. BuShag sensed something else in these paintings. There was a message in them. The characters the fisherman described had meaning, but what? The canoes full of men without faces: who? BuShag felt the painter or painters had left a message for her people, and it was very important. She decided she must see them.

She gathered herself, stepped out of the door to her hut, and shuffled down the path to where the rest of the community was busy with the spring day's activities. When they saw her coming, activities drew to a halt and small children went to stand beside their mothers. Some of the older boys were going to show their bravery by teasing or taunting the old woman, but the men quickly drew them aside. BuShag asked for the fisherman who had told her of the rock paintings discovered on their recent trip.

The man stepped forward with his nephew just behind him. BuShag lifted her bony arm and pointed a crooked finger at his chest. "You," she said, "must take me there, to the paintings. I must see the paintings." The man looked at her questioningly. Her people looked at each other with skepticism. Too old and frail, was the common but unspoken thought; she wouldn't travel well. BuShag perceived their reluctance to take her, and became more insistent. The location was part of the message she perceived from the paintings, she explained. Not wanting to further agitate the old medicine woman, the man agreed. He chose two others, as well as his nephew who had first seen the pictographs, and said they would make plans to leave early the next day.

They took two canoes for the trip, with BuShag squatting

in the middle of one, and the four men paddling. Traveling light, they moved very quickly. BuShag rode the portages on one of the men's backs, and there wasn't much conversation along the way. By the end of the second day they were only a couple lakes away from the site. They would see the paintings the next morning.

The morning came with thick, low clouds raking the ragged tops of the pines. The air was damp and chilled, and while they made their way to the lake where the paintings were, a fine mist hung in the air. When they reached the location, the men set up shelter nearby under their canoes, but BuShag insisted that the youth take her directly to the pictures. In a low spot by the water's edge, she squatted looking at the paintings at the base of a high overhanging rock face extending to her left. Both the horizontal and vertical angles of the rock face lead her eye along the waterline, along the row of painted images, down the length of the lake which extended to the east.

After a time the men coaxed a smoldering fire into being in spite of the damp wood, which hissed in protest under slow-motion flames. The men huddled under the canoes trying to stay warm and dry by their little fire, and mumbled to each other about what the old woman was learning, if anything, from the paintings on the rock. Why did these paintings seem so special to her?

That's the way the afternoon passed, and the evening. Periodically one of the men would venture down to the shore to see how BuShag was doing. Sometimes she would be squatting, gazing at the paintings, sometimes reaching up to touch them, running her hand over the wet surface of the rock. Other times she stood gazing to the east, beyond the far shore. She was soaked by the misty rain, and looked like a tiny drowned bird, yet seemed impervious to the weather. During this time she never stopped to take nourishment or rest, and said nothing to the men who waited above.

The drizzle let up mercifully as darkness fell, and the men kept the fire going for BuShag. But even though it was too dark to see the paintings she remained by them at the water's edge. Late into the night, the men were awakened by a moaning howl that ended in one of BuShag's long, eerie chants. It was a sad sound, deeply moving, though the words were unknown to the men. The lament went on and on, and despite the time of night no one could sleep.

Two of the men got up and went down to BuShag. She was standing with skinny arms uplifted, facing across the water with her face toward the sky. Her chant continued awhile longer, then she collapsed, shaking, to the ground. The two men picked her up and brought her to the shelter of the canoes and covered her with warm robes. She seemed asleep, but her eyes were open. They were all frightened. This must be an evil place, they decided, and they would head home with the first light of morning.

The journey back went even more swiftly than the journey to the lake, and BuShag spent it reclining in the bottom of the canoe, oblivious to her surroundings. Immediately on their return, BuShag was taken to her hut and covered with warm dry robes and fed warm broth. She seemed unresponsive, and had shivering episodes that lasted a long time. During these times BuShag would sometimes rant, saying strange things, using strange words. They thought she was talking with the spirits. A woman sat with her day and night, tending to her needs. Everyone in the village thought this was the end of BuShag. She was weak and frail to begin with, and her great age – well, the end seemed inevitable now. After several days of believing her death was imminent, the village held a ceremony to honor her spirit. Yet the old medicine woman lived on.

Six days she remained in this state, and on the seventh, she seemed to be more like herself, and spoke to the woman attending to her. In a couple more days, BuShag told the woman to leave her. Everyone was amazed at her recovery, but she seemed to have distanced herself from The People even more after her illness. No one saw her around the village anymore, and seldom outside of her hut. They brought food to her, but she rarely spoke to anyone. When she did, she was detached, as if she were not involved in the conversation.

BuShag had become preoccupied with the symbols on the rock painting, as she constantly scratched the various images in the dirt and mumbled to herself. Eventually, on a roll of birch bark, she drew out the entire pictograph from memory, with considerable accuracy and detail. She would sit for hours staring at it, pondering the meaning. Then, in meditation, she'd "speak to the spirits" about them.

This continued through the summer, and into the fall. Finally, in the time of the hunting moon, BuShag came into the village one evening just before dark. The people stopped what they were doing and came to her. She looked older than ever, and even more frail. In her dry, croaking voice that was weak from lack of use, she said that she now understood the paintings on the rock. She wanted to speak to the council as soon as possible.

After they were assembled, BuShag began with a short song for her people. She paused, and then began to talk about the paintings. She started by telling about their location and its significance, then described them in full detail, drawing the more complex images in the dirt. She then began to interpret them, explaining that they were indeed made by "the First Ones," those who had been in this land long before The People. The pictographs were a message from "the First Ones." She told those assembled that they, The People, had long ago "replaced" the older race that had been on the land in a time before. This older race was all gone now, and would never be again. BuShag explained that the pictures told of a new people who were coming. Those alive now would not live to see the new race, but perhaps their children, or grandchildren would. They would come from the east in canoes first, a few at a time, and then many. This new race would be easily recognized. They would have faces, but their faces were pale, like death. They would overtake the Earth Mother, and they would come to somehow own the land. They would bring sickness and death to the Earth Mother, destroying the forests and its creatures, poisoning the waters and tearing up the soil. Their medicine would be very powerful, and against their numbers, resistance would be futile. But BuShag told those assembled that The People must remain strong to survive, or like the ancient ones they had replaced, they would be swallowed up by the new race, the ones with no color. Then the People would be no more, and the Earth Mother would become very sick and perhaps die. To save the Earth Mother would be difficult, but it would be the only way for anyone to survive.

Now everyone at the assembly began talking with great concern. Some of the younger men might have passed off the words of BuShag as those of a ranting old woman, but no one had ever predicted the end of their world. The elders knew BuShag didn't often make predictions, but when she did they were usually accurate. Given BuShag's recent visits with the spirits after the discovery of the strange paintings, her words had even more credibility.

BuShag had spoken, but her message lacked a solution, and no one among the assembled men and elders of the village knew what to do. Other villages would never believe the tale, and only a few of them even knew of BuShag. They could not resist concepts which they could not comprehend. They didn't even know when the new race would start to arrive, but it was not predicted in their lifetime. There was only one among them whose age had spanned lifetimes.

BuShag could sense their concern, and began to speak again. Though she had no power to change what was to be, perhaps she could meet the new race with a message about the Earth Mother. A sign that would warn them not to destroy the earth that is mother to all living things. Soon winter would be upon them. She needed to travel to the east, where the new race would come from, and she needed to do it soon, before freeze up, before her medicine was no longer strong enough.

The assembly agreed, it had to be done. It would take many days of cold and difficult travel and they might not make it back before the winter ice locked the lakes, but there were no other suggestions for meeting the future. The elders asked for volunteers, two young men and two older, experienced men. Traveling over the icy water that time of year with unstable weather could be miserable as well as dangerous, and only the most skilled and reliable men were selected. The uncle of the youth who discovered the paintings was first to volunteer, but this time the youth would stay behind.

The next day provisions were gathered for the travelers, and the men began to prepare themselves. They would not be traveling as light this trip, considering their needs in cold weather. An extra robe was provided for BuShag.

After two days of preparation, the party set out early one crisp, clear fall morning – with BuShag bundled in the middle of one canoe like so much cargo. They paddled into the sunrise, east, and south, in the direction of the big water, the direction from which the new race was to come.

On the water the bark canoes traveled swiftly and they made good time. On the portages the extra robes, provisions and BuShag slowed them down, but no one complained. The men's feet were soaked in the freezing water every day, and after the second day of the trip a slow, cold and steady rain began to fall. After paddling in it for one day, they stopped to wait it out. It lasted two more days, and when it quit they continued.

That's how the trip went, over portages, across lakes and down rivers. BuShag rarely spoke, and seemed to be lost in her thoughts, which the men would not disturb. They believed she was with the spirits, working out what she was going to do. The men provided for her needs for food or assistance, in consideration of her great age, but she rarely asked for anything. Nights or layovers they spent under the shelter of the two canoes with a hide stretched between them if there was rain. They ate pemmican and dried fish or meat, wild rice and dried berries. A few times one of the men would get a rabbit or grouse along a portage and they'd have fresh meat. Then they'd boil the bones for a broth to give BuShag.

After about ten days of travel they made a long portage around a big waterfall, and continued down a river. The river emptied into the big water, now called Lake Superior. The day they arrived on the big lake it was windy, and huge waves crashed along the rocky shore. They sought shelter in the trees, and killed a deer to replenish their food supplies. The next day the wind had subsided, and they set off precariously on the big lake, hugging the shoreline but making good time.

After a couple days travel, the weather turned sour again. They put ashore by midday, and after sheltering their canoes they went inland and built a shelter for themselves under an overhanging rock formation. The weather intensified to a full-blown storm, with pelting rain and the icy wind heaving thunderous breakers against the huge rocks on the shore.

The party barely had time to fortify their shelter and gather dry wood, but they were relatively secure huddled next to the big rock. They sat close to the fire, covered in their robes to keep warm. The men took the opportunity to rest up from their arduous trip, but though she was exhausted BuShag could not, would not rest. With the intensity of the storm and the approach of winter, she knew her hour had come. Inside the shelter, she unwrapped her medicine bag, took out the items she needed and placed them in a small circle around her. Then BuShag began chanting and performing rituals which the men knew nothing about. It didn't matter to them. In their exhausted state neither the howling wind nor BuShag's activities kept them awake.

The remainder of the day BuShag carried on her ritual, chanting and weaving by the fire to the accompaniment of the howling wind and pounding surf. On into the night she continued, while the rain alternated as sleet or wet snow, illuminated by flashes of lightning and rumbling thunder. Finally she stopped. She stared into the flames a long while, and spoke a few strange words. Then she awakened the uncle of the youth, the one who had first told her of the paintings.

She told him he must take her to the shore of the lake. "Now?" was the question she saw in his eyes, while the storm raged around them. "Now," was BuShag's reply.

Stiff and sore, the man dutifully roused himself while the others slept on. They ventured out of the shelter into the storm but neither was quite prepared for its violence. BuShag could not stand or walk against the wind and pelting sleet, so the man carried her on his back, groping in the dark through the wind-lashed brush. Guided by the flashes of lightning and sound of the surf, they struggled through the trees and brush out onto a rocky point that jutted into the raging lake.

When they reached the end of the point, there was nothing on the jagged wet rocks to shelter them from the pounding, crashing surf. The man was afraid to set BuShag down for fear the wind would blow her away, but she slid herself from his back. She told him to go, that his work was done. Then, on her hands and knees she clawed her way against the wind and over the glazed rocks, until just above the water's edge she stopped. Wedging her legs into spaces between the rocks for support, BuShag raised her hands to the heavens and began her chanting again, weaving in the wind. The man watched, dumbfounded by her tenacity, and certain she was singing her death song. The waves crashed around her and spray covered her, yet she managed to stay there on the rock. Eventually he retreated into the trees for shelter from the punishing weather, but kept an eye on her. He knew she couldn't last long.

Several times the man went back out on the rock, thinking she might change her mind. Each time, in the flicker of lightning he could see her drenched, twisted little frame clinging to the rock, staring east into the darkness over the black stormy lake.

Eventually, numb with cold, the man had had enough. If she had come here to die, he had not. He withdrew into the trees and headed back to the shelter. Looking over his shoulder one last time, in a long flash of lightning he saw BuShag still perched on that barren, wave-washed rock. Then he fought his way back through the storm and woods.

Nearly frozen when he returned to the shelter, he managed to pile some wood on the dwindling fire before covering himself with dry robes. Still he shivered through the remainder of the night, unable to sleep.

Near morning, he dozed off, with strange men and strange creatures filling his restless dreams. He dreamed of BuShag, of ancient people and cliff paintings. He dreamed of men with pale faces, and BuShag was there to confront them. She would always be there.

The sky was light when he woke. The wind, rain and snow had stopped, but the ground outside the shelter was covered with wet, melting slush. He was still cold but felt better after building up the fire. The other men stirred, but were reluctant to move. Slipping out of the shelter the man made his way through the trees toward the rocky point where he had left BuShag in the storm. She'd certainly be dead, but perhaps he could find her body so they could properly care for it. When he stepped from the trees out onto the end of the point where he had left BuShag in the storm, there was no sign of her.

Instead there stood a small, twisted and bent old cedar tree with gnarled roots firmly clutching the spaces in the jagged, bare rock. The tree had not been there the night before. Slowly he understood that he would not find BuShag's body. He sat down on the roots of the old cedar as a child sits on its grandmother's knee. Gazing across the great lake toward the pale glow of the rising sun, he knew that those who came from the east would encounter the tree. And the tree would be there for a long, long time.

The Luckiest Man In The World

During the Second World War, Ernest Fortune survived the Pacific Campaign by an odd sort of luck. Ernest seemed to have more than his share of close calls, but in his own words was, "just damn lucky." His buddies, who called him Ernie, were in total agreement on that. But it was a form of luck the other soldiers were just as pleased to be without. For example, Ernie once single-handedly shot down an enemy plane, but barely managed to get clear before it crashed directly on the heavy machine gun he was using. Ernie miraculously escaped unharmed. That was his brand of luck. He saw a lot of action and returned home a bit "battle fatigued," but with a fresh perspective on life and what he wanted to do with it.

During the war, Ernie often sought refuge in his mind, where he kept the memories of better places, better times. He'd retreat from battle or boredom into the memories of serene sunsets over placid, pine-rimmed lakes that teemed with fish.

Ernie wasn't from the North Country; in fact he had grown up in a big city. He had accompanied his father and friends on a couple of fishing trips in the canoe country as a youth, and had always loved fishing and the outdoors. He devoured books on fishing and became, at least "by the book," quite learned on the various techniques of angling. More important, he was blessed with uncanny luck in being able to catch fish. While still in the South Pacific, Ernie decided that if he survived the war, he was going to become a fishing guide in the wilderness area of northeastern Minnesota. After separation from the army, he pooled his resources, which didn't amount to much, and in the early spring of 1946 headed that direction.

The Luckiest Man In The World

With no plan in mind, Ernie reached the Ely city limits at about the same time his car ran out of gas. The right front tire went flat as he got out to check the steaming radiator. He propped one foot on the bumper, which came loose with a jerk, and viewed the freshening spring forest around him. As he drew in a deep breath of pine-scented air, the car rolled from under his foot into the ditch where it got hung up on an outcropping of native bedrock. Ernie gazed toward the little town set in the midst of one of America's last great wilderness areas. "I must be the luckiest man in the world," he said to himself as thick clouds began to dump their heavy load.

It wasn't going to be easy, finding a position as a guide with one of the area resorts or outfitters. First of all, Ernie didn't fit the physical image of a robust outdoors man of the north woods. He was just under average height, and the stress of the war had left him so thin his clothes almost billowed around him. He wore a pair of army boots and his army khaki pants which puckered at the waist where his baggy Hawaiian-style sport shirt tucked in. His delicate jaw framed a boyish mouth that twitched slightly at the right corner when he was stressed, another residual effect of the war. He looked too young to have much credibility, until you looked into the eyes behind the glasses which rode halfway down his small nose. In those eyes one could see that Ernie had been to war, and he was a survivor. Besides, there was an air about him that suggested you might want to hang around because something interesting was going to happen with this guy, and you wouldn't want to miss it.

Besides Ernie's unlikely image, no one was hiring or they were all too busy to really talk, not that it mattered much to him. He was still floating with joy at just being in the lake country and eager to try his hand at fishing.

Not long after the ice was out on area lakes, Ernie walked down the driveway of the only resort in the area he hadn't called on yet, and inquired at the desk if he might speak to the owner. A woman, probably the owner's wife and more rugged in appearance than Ernie, told him "Harv" was putting in the dock and would be busy all day. Ernie headed straight for the dock and found "Harv", a big, powerful looking man, just out from shore in a boat full of pipes and tools. He was wrestling a long heavy pipe into upright position in the deep icy water.

A couple of dock sections were already in position, but the last section was the most difficult, especially while he was trying to avoid a bath in the ice cold lake. It was a sunny day and Harv, being rather heavy, was working up quite a sweat in the warm spring air. Ernie watched in silence. Finally the man seemed to have the pipe in position and paused, puffing and wheezing with sweat dripping down his face. He stared suspiciously at Ernie for a moment as he held onto the pipe to keep the boat in position, then said, "What can I do for ya?"

"I need a job," Ernie replied.

"Me too. 'Gotta pay for this place somehow. What can you do?" asked Harv as he stood up in the boat and grabbed the pipe with both hands as if he was ready to choke it.

"Well," said Ernie as he walked out onto the two dock sections that were in place, "I wanna be a guide, but right now it looks like you need a hand with this dock."

Harv was in a vulnerable situation, but eyed Ernie skeptically and told him he wasn't hiring. Having sized up the situation as a two-man job, Ernie replied cavalierly that it was OK, he'd just help the man get that last dock section in place. With that, he took a long, confident stride from the dock to the bow of the boat, as Harv yelled "NOOOOOOO!"

From that point, it all seemed to happen in slow motion. Ernie's lunge naturally pushed the boat away, catching both Ernie and the resort owner off guard. Harv suddenly became suspended precariously over an ominously dark, widening gap of water between the pipe he'd just imbedded in the lake bottom and the boat. Immediately off balance, Ernie fell into the rocking boat, skinning shins and knuckles, and unable to react quickly enough to help the suspended man.

From down in the bottom of the boat Ernie could hear the man groan through gritting teeth as the tilting pipe and the boat slid further away from each other. The air tingled with the intensity of the situation as Harv's stretched torso exposed his big, bare belly mere inches over the frigid lake surface. When neither air nor man could bear the tension any longer, he bellowed the first syllable of a curse before belly-flopping into the cold dark water.

Moments later, Harv stumbled up onto the rocky shore with bluish skin and teeth chattering so badly he'd have bitten his tongue off if he'd tried to speak. It was just as well he didn't, considering what was on his mind. Harv turned stiffly to glare at Ernie who, with glasses dangling from one ear and Yankees cap sideways, was still trying to right himself in the rocking boat. Cautiously, as though peering from a South Pacific foxhole, Ernie's eyes squinted at the backlit silhouette of the resort owner, whose cold, drenched clothing steamed in the warm spring air. With the bright morning sunlight behind him, Harv looked like a supernatural apparition. The corner of Ernie's mouth twitched uncontrollably as he managed to say, "Actually, I...I'm much better at fishing."

Harv tried to hold his icy stare, but seeing Ernie still struggling in the boat, the big man cracked a smile and began to laugh. He laughed long and hard and soon Ernie was laughing with him. Then big Harv invited Ernie to come up to the office for a cup of coffee.

Ruth, the woman behind the desk who was indeed Harv's wife, poured Ernie a cup while Harv got into some dry clothes. When he joined them and told Ruth what had happened, the laughing started all over again. The three of them got acquainted, swapping stories over coffee with Ruth's homemade biscuits and jam. Ernie felt as though he'd finally come home, and it was the beginning of a long friendship.

The resort really wasn't hiring; they couldn't afford to. Their former guide/hired hand had left Ruth and Harv since they couldn't afford to pay him. He had a drinking problem anyway, so Ruth was glad to see him go. Ernie eventually got around to telling them about his love of fishing and dream of being a guide, but admitted things just hadn't worked out yet. Ruth and Harv looked at each other in silence, then she spoke first. They really did need help, she said. Harv quickly explained that they had no money to pay him, but if he wanted to work awhile for room and board until business picked up they'd let him stay and give it a try. Ernie was delighted. This was a lucky day for the luckiest man in the world. They shook on it, and Ruth went to prepare a place for Ernie as the two men headed out the door to work. "I hope you are better at fishin'," Harv said as he clamped a big hand over Ernie's shoulder.

Well, Ernie was pretty good at finding good fishing spots, but he was unfamiliar with canoes, only somewhat familiar with handling boats, and knew nothing about outboard motors. Working closely with Harv, he learned how the motors worked and what it took to keep them running, just before the season opener.

One calm evening, Ernie thought he'd better take a boat out and familiarize himself with the lake before guests started arriving. Ruth and Harv helped him get prepared and launched him from the dock. After a few pulls on the rope Ernie had the motor chugging and sputtering in a cloud of blue outboard exhaust, but it wasn't running smoothly. Ernie had seen Harv adjust the mixture many times to make the engine hum evenly, so he knew what to do. He stood up and leaned over the back of the boat to find the screw adjustment and the motor sputtered as though it was about to stall. Without thinking, Ernie reached for the throttle to give it more gas and...

Well, of course Ruth and Harv were watching from the dock and could see it all. As Ernie hit the throttle the boat shot out from under him. He turned a perfect half-gainer in midair before landing in the wake of his empty boat which was headed for the open water of the lake. He resurfaced to the fading drone of the outboard and the rising, roaring laughter from the dock. Harv was avenged.

It was an appropriate way to open the coming season, as Ernie's efforts often resulted in mishap at his own expense. Ruth and Harv winced when he tipped over while turning to wave good-bye as the group pulled away on the first canoe trip he guided. Needless to say that didn't instill confidence in the party from St. Louis, setting out on their first wilderness fishing trip. But Ernie brought them back safely, and with a wealth of stories to tell, many of them about Ernie.

On the next canoe trip, however, Ernie lost the compass over the side and had neglected to bring a spare. Those folks had an extended trip at no extra cost, as it took

Ernie two days longer to find his way back. Luckily, fishing was good.

With all these incidents, Ruth and Harv became concerned about whether or not Ernie was going to work out as a fishing guide. But somehow, fishing was always good with Ernie. He always knew where to fish and how to catch them. As the season went on, they noted that everyone was coming back in good health and humor, and many even scheduled a trip for the next year. It wasn't despite Ernie, but because of Ernie that they were having such good times.

Ernie's attitude about life and way with people seemed to turn uncertain situations into golden moments. People enjoyed their trips with Ernie no matter what happened, and one never knew what was going to happen around Ernie. His reactions made their experiences special. Ernie felt things would always worked out for the best, and maybe that feeling just rubbed off on people.

Once a fishing party of Milwaukee businessmen on their first trip with Ernie, came to the bottom of a rapids which they needed to portage around to get to the lake above. Ernie went first, shouldering his pack and then his canoe. It was a short portage which followed the rushing flow of the stream at high water that time of the year. Ernie enjoyed portaging, often stopping to admire a nice rapids or blooming plant which would remind him of how lucky he was to be working in such a beautiful area. He set his canoe in the water at the top of the portage, dropped his pack inside and hurried back to help the others.

They made a couple trips over the portage, carrying everything they had, and were about to set out when Ernie noticed his canoe was missing. He was sure some of the fishermen in the party were playing a trick on him, but they swore they were not. Finally someone asked where he had set it when he brought it across. Puzzled, he stared at the spot, then slowly looked up and beyond to the top of the rapids. It dawned on him that he didn't recall securing his canoe before returning to help the others. His eyes got real big, and a short, high-pitched noise came from his twitching mouth as he turned to dash back down the portage trail. About 20 minutes later Ernie returned to his waiting party. He was soaking wet, carrying a slightly dinged-up canoe and a very soggy pack which streamed water through a small hole in the bottom. Without a word he set the canoe in the water, placed the heavy, still-draining pack inside the canoe, got in and paddled off.

It didn't take long to figure out what had happened, but nobody said anything until that evening. That's when the real fun began. The men started creating stories about how that canoe and pack got back down the portage and how Ernie got soaking wet – stories other than the obvious one, that is. They were extraordinary concoctions, wild speculations, too fantastic to be true. But Ernie himself would have preferred to believe any of them rather than what had actually happened – the guide, actually leaving his canoe and pack unsecured at the top of a rapids.

After that trip, Ruth and Harv thought for sure they'd seen the last of the men from Milwaukee. Instead, they made the trip with Ernie an annual event. Each year one of them called to make early reservations, and each year they specifically requested that Ernie be their guide. And each year became enriched with more episodes.

One year stories had been circulating in the area about how some of the more intrepid guides were hitching rides on swimming moose. According to the stories, if a moose was seen swimming across a lake, as they sometimes do, the guide – who was to ride the moose – rode in the bow of a canoe, and a second man paddled right behind him, and a third man in the stern. The three would paddle as fast as they could to overtake the moose. They'd paddle right up next to the churning beast, and at the right moment the guide would leap from the canoe onto the animal's mostly submerged back. This of course panicked the huge creature, defenseless in the deep water, and the rider had to hang on for dear life. The men left in the canoe would paddle to stay close, so they could get between man and beast to rescue the guide when he got off the moose. It was a very risky and stupid thing to do, and undoubtedly caused a great deal of unnecessary stress and aggravation to the moose.

Well, Ernie's Milwaukee buddies got wind of these stories just before heading out for a week of fishing. This sort of macho display was just what they expected from a "real" woodsman, a "real" guide. Oh, they allowed that Ernie knew his fishing all right, but... well, it was that image thing. Toward the end of the trip they had practically convinced Ernie that among guides at every resort in the area, moose were the preferred means of transport. He was probably the only guide who hadn't ridden one. Now Ernie wasn't particularly gullible and took the prodding in stride, but he'd heard the stories too. By the end of the week, after some consideration, Ernie was convinced that it not only could be done, but he could do it. With the hearty approval of the Milwaukee businessmen, he agreed that if they found a swimming moose in the last couple days of the trip, he'd ride it.

As Ernie's luck would have it, while they were paddling the last day of the trip they did indeed spot a moose crossing a lake. They paddled like mad men, with shouts of bravado and encouragement on Ernie's behalf. Finally, after extreme effort, they overtook the moose. It was a

young bull of formidable size with small antlers in vel-
vet. The whites of the animal's eyes shone, and it was
undoubtedly terrified. Ernie was already riding an adren-
aline high at this point, pumped and ready. His eyes were
wide too, and the corner of his mouth twitched so much
he couldn't form words to express how excited he was.
His canoe pulled alongside, and with accompanying
whoops and cheers Ernie leaped for the moose, almost
swamping the canoe in the process. It was perfect, just as
he imagined it. Ernie grabbed handsful of wet moose
hair and felt his legs straddle the flanks of the animal, at
about the same time that the moose felt the lake bottom
near shore where a point jutted into the lake. With solid
footing, the great beast wasted no time scrambling up
the rocks and into the tag alder with Ernie astride. Ernie,
eyes bulging and mouth contorted in a spasm, clung to
the moose for dear life. He was afraid to let go and get
off, not knowing what the moose would do to him. The
Milwaukee businessmen had stopped paddling and were
gliding along now in stunned silence. Nobody had been
paying attention to how close they were getting to shore.
The men sat in disbelief, listening to the sound of crashing brush and Ernie's frantic cries of "WHOA!" and
"HEEELP!" fading in the distance.

They looked at each other in dumbfounded silence. They
waited nearly four hours, not wanting to leave the area,
not wanting to return without Ernie, not wanting to try
explaining to Ruth and Harv. The men took turns going
ashore into the thick brush looking and calling for him.
There was a sense of guilt among them, of being somehow responsible for the tragedy. If Ernie ever was found,
they were certain it would be long after he was dead. It
was a somber group that kept vigil there, and several
heads were bowed, presumably in prayer. Finally, they
decided a canoe with two men should go for help while

the rest stayed to look and wait for Ernie. As the two men were about to leave, a faint voice was heard calling several hundred yards down the lake shore. It was Ernie. With shouts of relief the elated men paddled hard to meet him.

He was sitting in the lake bathing away the mud and soothing a multitude of scrapes, scratches and bruises. His clothes were torn and his face was drawn and haggard, as it must have looked after a battle in the South Pacific. He looked like he'd been to hell and back a second time.

The men greeted him with choruses of "Boy, are we glad to see you!," "What happened?" and "Are you ok?" The corner of his mouth still twitched a little as Ernie said, "Yeah, I think so. Just help me in the canoe." One of the men said, "Man, we thought you were a goner for sure. Where have you been?" Ernie, trying to cover his relief with nonchalance, replied, "Oh, I had a little unfinished business in St. Paul to take care of."

With good humor restored, the men loaded him into the middle of a canoe. Ernie duffed the rest of the way back to the resort, riding like an honored warrior, a genuine hero. Reclining in the canoe he reviewed what had just happened with the moose and for some reason recalled his war experiences. Once again he felt lucky to be alive. Maybe he was the luckiest man in the world after all. There was a smile on his face as he fell into an exhausted sleep between the packs.

That episode firmly entrenched Ernie in the hearts of this Milwaukee bunch, and they became his most loyal clients over the years.

About that time Coleman gas stoves were becoming popular with many campers. Ernie quickly perceived the value of cooking with "white gas" on the canoe trails. It was fast and clean, and you didn't have to worry about gathering and splitting wood or keeping it dry. The gas stoves weren't as romantic as cooking over a fire, and a fire is fine for a one-week trip. But if you were a guide and you cooked outdoors all summer, the Coleman gas stove was like the re-discovery of fire, more important than manned flight; like the electrification of rural America. With the gas stove, Ernie found he actually had a little time to relax on a trip, and he did have to work as hard. Yes, the stove was heavy and he had to carry fuel cans, but to Ernie's way of thinking it was well worth it.

But the convenience of the gas stove didn't necessarily mean more creative cooking. Ernie remained a traditionalist when it came to trail food, preferring the old staples of beans and dehydrated or dried foods, which tend to take the kinks out of the digestive tract. While very healthy, this high-fiber diet often induces a considerable degree of flatulence among most folks. In the wilderness, the occasional indiscretion of that sort may be overlooked, but toward the end of one trip the extremes of Ernie's menu actually began affecting the morale of the party. The rumblings became verbal protests, suggesting that the healthy diet was possibly more "benefit" than a modern man's system could tolerate, (with the exception of the fish, of course). Some claimed Ernie's cooking required the four stomachs of a bovine to properly digest it. Ernie took it in stride and thought it was just more good-natured ribbing. He actually believed that, like granny's old cod liver oil treatment, the diet was just what that Milwaukee Bunch needed.

In those years, the Forest Service was beginning to put, for lack of a more delicate term, "crappers" at a number of the more heavily used campsites. These crude toilet facilities were just rough, pre-cut lumber nailed together as a box with a hinged lid, and placed over a hole dug in the earth. Nothing fancy, but a necessary move to keep the woods around the camp sites more sanitary.

One warm summer day near the end of a trip along the Kawishwi route, a Milwaukee man named Norm came back down the path from the toilet and commented that the warm weather really made that place stink. He wasn't the first to complain either, as nearly everyone returned from the "crapper" short of breath.

Ernie was putting the cooking things away after breakfast. He had wished there was something he could do about the offensive odor too, but had been at a loss. As Ernie was busy, Norm commented, mostly to himself, that perhaps he had an idea that might help. Seizing the gas can he headed back up the malodorous path.

Later as Ernie was putting the stove away, he picked up the gas can and noted it was empty. No problem. He had another can and the trip was nearly over. Yeah, that stove was pretty slick.

Everyone else was almost ready to go fishing, but Ernie had one last matter that needed attending before setting out on the lake. He grabbed the roll of toilet paper from a pack and headed up the path to the latrine. Dropping his pants he sat himself upon the wood box "throne." This was a guide's one rare moment of peace and solitude on a canoe trip, a time when he wasn't likely to be disturbed. A time to relax. Ernie sighed, and as it was his habit, lit up a cigarette and sat there serenely enjoying the view of the lake and the great pine forest. It was a beautiful day in a beautiful world, and they were soon going to be fishing. His work was his play in a magnificent playground. Bathed there in the dappled sunlight and caressed by soft forest breezes, Ernie felt he most certainly was the luckiest man in the world.

Back in camp one of the men broke the spell, yelling,

"Hey Ernie, what's tak'n you so long. We've got a date with some lunkers." Finishing his business, Ernie cinched up his pants and casually tossed the cigarette butt down the hole of the crapper.

The first thing to reach camp was a dimly filtered flash, followed immediately by a loud "WHUMP!" That was followed closely by Ernie, though the men didn't recognize him at first. He was covered with reeking latrine contents as he dashed past the baffled Milwaukians. He ran full tilt into the lake and stayed under for a long time. Finally he pulled himself onto a rock at the shoreline and squinted in the sunlight at the men who gathered with puzzled expressions and pinched nostrils. "Okay, you win," Ernie gasped with his mouth a-twitch, "I'll change the menu."

There was only one thing that Ernie didn't care for in the canoe country, and that was bears. Bears not only put fear in Ernie's heart; he just plain disliked them. They caused destruction and trouble on a trip. But bears are a part of this area. If one spends any time at all here, one will inevitably encounter a bear. Just the sight of one set Ernie's mouth to twitching. When others wanted to take pictures of them, he was always ready to push on.

One season near the end of June, Ernie and the Milwaukee bunch were on a lake that was suffering from too many walleye and not enough fishermen. Their campsite, while otherwise perfect, was known to be plundered regularly by a large, gluttonous bruin that was bold, cunning and arrogant. Ernie disliked the idea of camping there, but it was the best location on the lake and there was no finer fishing to be found.

The bear in fact, did invite himself to breakfast one morning, and cleaned up the pancakes, batter, bacon, and butter, and then finished off his snack by tipping up a bottle of syrup and guzzling the whole thing. Obviously, the ol' boy had practiced this routine before. Ernie and one of the other men nervously gathered up the other food in a flash and paddled it to safety. The rest of the group harassed the offensive intruder until, finding nothing else properly prepared to his taste, he left.

The next afternoon, the men were having great fun swimming after successfully fishing a "hot spot" Ernie had found. Ernie decided to let them enjoy the fun while he took the catch back to camp early to clean them for supper. It didn't take him long to clean the fish and get things ready, but the boys were still out swimming and sunning themselves.

Now in those early days, the "Milwaukee Bunch" was inclined to bring along a quantity of an elixir for the prevention of snake bite and promotion of good will overall. Usually it was a Canadian distillation. The stuff proved to be excellent against snake bite, as none of them ever succumbed to the effects of that misfortune, at least not on any of Ernie's trips.

Noting the full jug of "medicinal whiskey" in the kitchen box, Ernie poured himself a dose and decided to relax until the crew came back. Stretching out on a well-contoured rock ledge he tilted his cap low over his eyes. As he tossed back the last swallow from the tin cup, Ernie reflected on his life as he often did in peaceful moments. Many men paid good money to come to this country and do what he did for a living. Yeah, I'm a lucky man for sure, thought Ernie, as he dozed off.

Meanwhile, the opportunistic bear had just been waiting until Ernie had cleaned all the fish before sauntering into camp to dine. The big brute padded right past Ernie's prostrate form and in less time than it takes to tell it he devoured all the fish.

Looking for something to wash down the meal, the bear noticed the familiar form of a bottle left sitting on the kitchen box. With the crude manners of a skid row bum, that bear dexterously pulled the cork with its teeth and spit it aside. Then, as with the pancake syrup, he up-ended the bottle and drained it – the entire jug of Canadian "snake bite tonic."

Emitting a gurgling, boozy belch, the bear glanced around for something else to eat. Unaccustomed to alcohol, the onset of its effects came on quickly.

Who knows what the world looks like to a besotted bruin, but no doubt his poor vision was first to suffer. The bear tried to stand on its hind legs and promptly rolled over. It got up on all fours and stumbled, tripping over its own feet. Eventually, it slumped down beside Ernie and passed out.

That's the way the fishermen found them, Ernie and the bear sleeping side by side. With a long stick, one of the men poked at Ernie to wake him. Ernie reacted by swinging his arm and giving the bear a smack on the snout with his hand. Immediately Ernie sensed something wasn't quite normal. He sat bolt upright at the same time the bear did. For a moment they were nose to nose, blinking at each other without comprehending. Then Ernie let out a shriek and the bear a bleating bellow as they scrambled to get away from each other. The men who were gathered around closely, now scattered in panic, yelling and looking for shelter.

In the commotion, Ernie tripped over a log bench and knocked the wind out of himself. The bear staggered backwards and fell over several times before running into a tree. Getting up again, it ran into a tent that one of the fishermen had just dived into. The bawling bear became frantic, probably thinking it was caught by something, and shredded the tent trying to escape. The fisherman, his head under a sleeping bag, miraculously escaped unscathed. The drunken bear headed for the woods, walking sideways, falling down and bumping into trees.

While straightening up later, the men found the empty whiskey bottle, and sized up what had happened. They accused Ernie of getting the bear drunk. Ernie said that the event reminded him of a bad date he'd been on once, but declined to elaborate.

That night, they listened to fits of pitiful bawling from the inebriated bear crashing about some distance off in the surrounding woods. The morning after, no doubt suffering an incredible hang over, the poor bear probably took the pledge. Having learned a hard lesson about intemperance and the human diet, it never returned to their camp, and apparently quit the area for good.

As years went by, the canoe country got more crowded. Oh, it was still beautiful to Ernie, and he continued to do well fishing and guiding for Ruth and Harv, but he was growing restless. He didn't want to move; he was just looking for something different, some sort of change. He found it in the local talk about trophy fish being hauled in from the lakes in Northern Ontario. Of course, those lakes were so remote you had to fly in.

To Ernie, that sort of a trip re-kindled the original romance he'd felt when he first came to the canoe country. It combined the adventures of exploring "untapped wilderness" and testing new waters for that "ultimate catch." He made it his business to get acquainted with a bush pilot who flew fishing parties into Ontario, and before August was half gone, Ernie made a fly-in trip up there to one of those dark crystal gem lakes.

It was perfect. The drizzly weather, the hordes of bugs,

the bountiful fishing – everything about the trip was too good to be true. Ernie was hooked. He made plans with the pilot for the coming season, and even started lining up clients. It wasn't that he didn't plan to guide for Ruth and Harv anymore, it was just his boyish enthusiasm for adventure and the sort of life Ernie loved. Ruth recognized it, but had to help Harv understand.

That next summer, sometime in the mid 1950s, Ernie started working the Canadian fly-in trips with his pilot friend. When he was back, he'd visit Ruth and Harv, but it was different, and they knew it. Sure he was the same Ernie, but when he talked about those far northern lakes he'd get that look in his eye that said that's where his heart was. He told them about a fly-in he and his pilot buddy were going on to scout a new Canadian lake they'd heard about. They'd be leaving the next weekend, Ernie said.

And so they did. With a canoe lashed to the pontoon struts, the two men and their gear lifted off the water shortly before sunup, headed for Canada. They were gone for a week, and then two. Sometime during the third week an air search was conducted, but nothing was found. Canadian bush pilots, fishermen and local Indians were questioned, but none of them had seen the little float plane or any sign of a wreck. As the weeks drew on, Ruth and Harv gradually accepted the fact that the men were not coming back. Perhaps Ernie's luck had finally run out.

But then, for all we know, Ernie is probably up there right now, gazing across a perfect northern lake surrounded by scented pines. If he is, he's no doubt casting a lure into a likely spot, and still thinking he's "the luckiest man in the world."

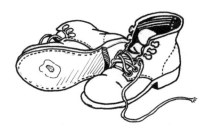

Wendigo

"Coreen...! Customer," he bellowed from behind the cash register as I blew through the doorway in a flurry of snow. The cold draft leafed through yesterday's newspaper lying on the counter and I headed for a stool at the far end, away from the door.

"Never mind Coreen, I got it," he rumbled, as I settled down with a sigh. Without looking at me, he said, "Hope you ain't come to eat, we just shut down the grill." It was late, and he seemed relieved when I told him I just wanted coffee and pie if he had any.

I made him out to be the owner of the diner, an average sized man with a more than average belly that hung over an apron spattered with the day's menu. His t-shirt was well past the 3000 mile oil change, and had a pack of cigarettes rolled up in the left sleeve. With his thinning greased hair, he brought to my mind a middle-aged, overweight James Dean.

"All I got left is one piece o' banana cream," he droned, placing a white mug of black, steaming coffee in front of me, "and somma yesterday's doughnuts. 'Least I think they're yesterday's."

I told him I'd have the pie, but noted that a fly behind the glass seemed to be avoiding it.

I'd been driving in the dark for several hours through an early winter snowstorm, on a trip that brought me to northern Minnesota and a town I hadn't been back to in nearly 40 years. It had been my father's town, and just seeing its name on a road sign awakened fond memories of glorious times spent in the surrounding lakes and woods. When my father moved away from the area, part of him stayed behind, and I guess a part of me stayed there with him. He never made it back.

The road was lonely and driving conditions poor, so I'd stopped for a break in the little town where I thought light, warmth and other people might lighten my load. My father's old home town. Maybe it wasn't just nostalgia but a restless feeling over unresolved issues that had somehow brought me back to find something we'd both left behind there.

Gazing wearily through the fogged front window of the diner, I ate the piece of pie. Inoffensively bland, it didn't remind me much of bananas, but the coffee tasted good. Maybe it was just hot. My thoughts continued to whirl and drift like the colored snowflakes in the light of the neon bar sign across the street.

"Yah, you go ahead Coreen, I'll close-up tonight," he called to the kitchen. "I'll hang around for the bar crowd. Yah, no problem. See ya t'morra. Drive careful!" Turning to me, he said, "Lemme heat that up for ya," and he filled my cup before ducking back into the kitchen.

A stirring in a dark corner caught my attention, and I swiveled on my stool to see a pile of rags haul itself from a back booth and take on human form. 'Til then, I'd thought the owner and I were the only warm bodies left in the place. I watched the figure become a man of huge proportions who stood unsteadily a moment before shuffling toward me in sloppy-fitting old Sorel boots. He wore a tattered, threadbare mackinaw with the collar held up by a long, burlap-looking scarf which hung like a dingy, dark curtain. His baggy bib overalls, which were worn and torn far beyond functional purpose, only partially covered layers of other old pants in similar condition. Shreds of cloth were tied around the legs to patch holes or hold things together, or maybe for insulation. From under a dirty wool logger's cap, matted hair stuck out in dull-nickle spikes. By his dark, deeply furrowed face I guessed he might be an Indian of late middle-age.

It seems every town has at least one of these characters I thought, but usually not as big. He lumbered my way heading toward the door, and I concentrated my stare into my coffee cup, hoping he would somehow get the message that I didn't want to be bothered. As though sensing my uneasiness, he paused towering behind me and changed course for the stool next to mine.

I didn't want to acknowledge his presence, but I could tell he was studying me. The owner of the diner was busy behind the counter putting glasses away, unaware of our developing encounter. I could sense eyes staring into me, carefully reading me, and taking my measure.

He brought with him a most peculiar odor that caught my attention. Though I couldn't identify it, the aroma wasn't necessarily unpleasant. After an uncomfortable moment I turned to confront the huge derelict and our eyes met. They weren't the glazed, jaundiced eyes I expected. Wild to be sure, their look was intelligent and penetrating, not dulled by booze or drugs. I saw something else also reflected in their clarity – a very confused man.

He spoke first. "I know you," he said in a deep, rich voice. "I'm certain I know you. We used to know each other I'm sure. Long time ago. D'you remember me? I know you from somewhere."

Caught off guard by his friendly manner, I replied that I was pretty sure I didn't know him at all, but for some reason my voice didn't sound convincing, even to me. I became aware that the concentration of his gaze took an instant hold of me, almost like a spell.

"Oh, you maybe don't recall right now, I don't either. But I know you somehow, from somewhere," he insisted. "I feel it in my bones. I know you, and you know me." His words came out easily and unhurried, but with the same intensity I saw in his eyes.

I forced myself to turn from him and sipped some coffee, but he persisted. "You ain't from around here, I know everybody around here," he said. "What brings you t'this neck-a-the-woods?"

"You're right," I admitted, "I'm not from around here, I'm just passing through, and you don't know me." I made a point of not mentioning that I'd spent a lot of time in the area when I was a kid. Conversation with a local who looked and talked like he might be certifiably crazy was not the relief I'd pulled off the road to find.

He chuckled a bit, and continued, "Oh yeah, I know you all right. We never met, but we know each other well enough. Not that it matters, but my name's Charlie. I don't expect that t'mean a thing t'you."

It didn't.

"Most folks 'round here know who I am, an' nearly every one of 'em is pretty well convinced I'm a log or two short of a full cord," Charlie said. I gave him a sideways glance, but didn't reply.

"That's OK, 'cause they don't know where I been. Folks 'round here don't know you either, an' they don't know where you been. I do. I know because I been there. I know you, 'cause once – I was you."

I winced at the remark, but now thought it best to not reply at all. If I could just ignore him maybe he'd leave me alone. At least there was no one else in the diner to witness my uneasiness. Even the owner had found something to do in the kitchen.

"What I mean is, I been in your place," he continued, "an' I know why you're here, why you've come back. Yah, I know. I came back too, long time ago. Something just made me, kept callin' me sort of. It was like nothin' in my life worked right for years, 'til I finally came back here to where I belong. It's where you belong too."

It wasn't working. I wasn't ignoring him. Even more unsettling was that what he was saying almost seemed to mean something to me. I couldn't figure out what it was, but for some reason his crazy babbling was reaching a place in my mind where it… had some sort of significance. A strange feeling was coming over me as he spoke in those deep, even tones.

"You've come home, that's what it is. Oh I ain't talkin' 'bout this town, this town ain't my home either. It's more about this area ain't it," Charlie said. "You feel a part of this land, and it's a part o' you. You never felt quite right, never were quite right when you was somewhere else. You and me, we're s'posed t'be here… with this land. You came back to be close to this part of the earth. It's called you here. Not by your name, but by your soul."

I remained silent, but he knew I was listening. I couldn't help it, it felt reassuring, like he was saying just what I wanted to hear.

"It don't matter what I say to most folks, they think I'm crazy anyhow," Charlie went on. "They don't take me seriously. But you know me, and I know you want to be a part of the seasons here, attuned to the weather, the sun and the moon. You want to feel the strength of the earth through the things that grow here; you want to run with the pack or fly with the flock. Some of us belong to the lakes and trees here. Other folks might have similar feelings to a degree, but not like you do, not like us.

"I remember the way it was, when things were simpler and everybody lived close to the earth. Now most folks go into the woods for just a visit. The government has to tell them folks how to behave when they go to the woods, and reminds 'em they're just visitors.

"Some folks have learned to believe the woods is a scary place with dangerous beasts an' all. They feel safer in a city with beasts o' their own kind, and a different set o' laws. They feel at home with a way of life that has got so messed up it's ruining the earth we share, our true home.

"You and me, we know better. When you go to the woods, you're no visitor, you're goin' home... back home... back to our Mother.

"C'mon, let's go," he said, "what're we doin' here. Let's go home."

I was ready. More than ready, I was mesmerized like a kid listening to a bedtime story and about to be carried off sleepily to bed. My state of mind must have been vulnerable, and his words and voice hypnotic. I'd lost my sense of reason, wasn't even sure where I was. I was just ready to go – somewhere.

Just then there was a loud noise in the kitchen as some kettles or something clanged and clattered to the floor followed by vociferous cursing. Distracted and confused, I swiveled on my stool and looked toward the kitchen doorway. There was a few more loud banging sounds as kettles were replaced on racks, and then the owner came through the kitchen door.

"Howya' doin' out here? Can I getcha anything else? Another refill?" he said in a voice that seemed to boom in the silence, but probably wasn't all that loud. At the same time I felt a draft and turned to see the front door to the diner just closing, and the newspaper shuffling again. The only thing remaining of Charlie was that peculiar odor lingering faintly before being overpowered by the smell of greasy cooking.

"Uh, no thanks, thanks anyway," I replied still recovering as though from a dream. "I really need to be going," I said rising from my stool. As we walked together toward the end of the counter near the front door where the cash register was, I said, "Say, who was that big guy that was sitting in the back booth when I came in? Some sort of local color?"

"You're the only customer I've had in over an hour," the owner replied, "there ain't been nobody else."

"Yeah," I said, "you know. Ragged looking Indian fella, really huge. You couldn't help but notice him."

"No, 'fraid not," the owner said looking back there, and then at me, "I got a buzzer that goes off in the kitchen when somebody comes in the door. I'd have noticed it on a slow night like this. 'Specially a big Indian."

"But I was talking to him here for quite awhile," I insisted. Apparently the guy couldn't hear us, it was a quiet conversation.

"Whatever you say pal, but I never saw anybody," he said again. "That'll be $3.89."

As I pulled a five spot from my wallet I noticed the name of the diner on a sign by the cash register that read: "Make checks payable to Wendigo Cafe."

"Wendigo Cafe," I read aloud. "I see that word every now and then around here. Just what does 'Wendigo' mean," I asked.

"Well," he said with a grin, "it's a Indian thing I guess. Tourists like that stuff ya know, an' it's just supposed to add some character to the name. Besides, it was named that before I took the place over years ago, and I thought it sounded fine so I never changed it."

"Yeah, it's a good enough name," I assured him, "but I was just wondering if you knew what a 'Wendigo' is."

He folded his arms over his belly and assumed an authoritative stance, obviously pleased to show his knowledge of a bit of local folklore, especially since it was connected to his business.

"I guess I can tell you as much as I know, and I don't know the whole thing or even if it's accurate. It's just a story," he began modestly.

"The Wendigo is from an old Indian legend that used to be told many years ago 'round these parts. The way I understand it, the Indians claimed this creature was part man, part moose and part... who knows – it's a legend. The Wendigo had red eyes that glowed in the dark, and it left smoldering hoof prints on the ground in the woods where it walked. It had a smell, like nothin' else you ever smelt anywhere. It smells something like... decayed leaves or wet earth, only smokey, or like a swamp, or... I don't know how to describe it, I never smelt it. It don't smell like nothin' else. Anyway, the Wendigo would come for a person, and when it did, it was irresistible. It came on the wind, and eventually you'd have to go with it, to run off into the woods, running like the wind and following it wherever it goes. It knows you, it comes looking for you, and you just hafta go. That's all I know about the Wendigo, and I guess it's something like that anyhow."

I stood there looking blankly at him. "Something like that," I thought to myself. At that moment, I was very confused, like a man caught between two worlds, not sure to which one he belonged.

Finally he reached out his hand and quietly said, "Here's your change. Have a good evenin', an' be careful on them roads now." I nodded, then buttoned my coat and pulled up the collar, before heading out into the weather.

As I stepped out the door of the Wendigo Cafe, a strong gust of wind buffeted me and howled in the nearby pines. For just a moment, I'm sure I could smell Charlie again.

The Story Of Jaque LaBeque

Jaque LaBeque was a hard man accustomed to a hard life trapping in the lake country of the Canadian Shield over 100 years ago. He cared little for the woods, but recognized its rich treasure in the furs. The mink, ermine, otter, fisher, martin, even muskrat and beaver were like living gold to him. LaBeque was obsessed with cashing in their pelts for as much money as he could before moving on to some other area or scheme. As a man, he was without ethics, conniving and and greedy. As a trapper, LaBeque was ruthlessly efficient, unencumbered by sentiment or compassion. He ran such long trap lines that animals caught at the beginning suffered a long time before he got back to collect them. Sometimes while held in a trap, an animal in pain and desperation would gnaw off its own leg or paw to escape. Of course the loss frustrated LaBeque, so he would extend his trapping even further. He never seemed to catch enough.

LaBeque sometimes would cross trap lines to take animals caught in other men's traps, and trappers watched their pelts whenever LaBeque was around. There wasn't much law around then, so there was little other trappers could do about LaBeque. Besides being hard to catch, LaBeque was a pretty rough customer. He was quick with the knife he used for skinning out furs, and violence came easy for him. More than one trapper with a heavy load of furs had "disappeared" on the trail, and no one dared confront the treacherous LaBeque about it.

But LaBeque wasn't without a friend. He occasionally shared a cabin with a malleable-minded half-breed named Claude Two Crows. Two Crows was a taciturn man accustomed to being alone. He was one of the few men in the area who occasionally trapped bear, since he was big and powerful enough to handle the huge traps. The scars of too close a scuffle with one bear had altered his countenance so it was impossible to tell whether he wore a permanent grimace or a grin. Two Crows cared nothing about LaBeque's personal ambitions, but had a weakness for trade rum. When Claude was in a thirsty mood, a bottle of rum would buy his services, including any dirty work LaBeque wanted done. Together they had wronged nearly every trapper in the area, and their reputations were well known among whites and Indians alike.

One cold, dark winter LaBeque and Two Crows were running traps in the Hunter's Island area. Returning from a couple days out on the line, they huddled by the stove in their drafty little log cabin. LaBeque cursed the cold and complained about the miserable life in this harsh land. Two Crows cursed too because it was his nature, so LaBeque assumed he felt the same way. That was why he included Two Crows in on a daring plan he had been considering since earlier that fall. He needed Two Crow's help.

Since fall LaBeque had been secretly mapping out a route in his mind that covered every trapper's line they knew of. They got supplies from the trading post for a long trek by dog sled, and let it be known that they were going on an extended trip to cover their trap lines, which they would do. But together, he and Two Crows would collect every pelt they could from every other trapper, and head for a trading post out of their area to cash them in.

Both men knew they'd be unable to return because every trapper would know who robbed them, and would be hunting for them. But with the money they would make from such a big load of furs, they wouldn't need to return. Besides, LaBeque's bad reputation was making it harder to cheat other men in the area, and it was time to move on.

After preparations, LaBeque and Two Crows set out early one bitterly cold January morning. Sundogs hounded the reluctant, pallid disk over the frozen horizon, and its pale light turned ice crystals in the air into a glittering fog. LaBeque and Two Crows urged their eager dogs down the trail with only a croaking raven to note their departure.

Before long they were following their trap line, quickly pulling frozen animals from traps before moving down the line. When they came across another trapper's trail, they'd follow it, collecting the prizes from every trap they found. Sometimes they split up, leap-frogging along the trail to cover the line more quickly. Haste was all-important to LaBeque, and everything was going smoothly. So smoothly he began to develop an odd, if ironic, sort of resentment in having to stop along the way and pick up the trapped animals. He kept reminding himself that they were the reason behind the whole scheme.

Things were going almost too well for LaBeque and Two Crows. Their sleds were getting heavy with the furs, and the dogs worked hard. Both men used their whips if the pace slowed. This was going to be the richest haul either had ever seen, and they talked about the price the furs would bring when they cashed them in. Yes, all was going according to plan, and their scheme was working well.

Over a week passed, and they were on the most remote part of their trip. At night, while their tired dogs slept, LaBeque and Two Crows laughed beside their fire as the northern lights danced, and wolves howled in the distance.

But the strain of their growing load was slowing their progress, and luck and provisions began to run out about the same time. One night as they slept, a pack of wolves came, killing one dog, and injuring two others before they chased them off. One of the injured dogs had to be shot. The next day, they discovered that another trapper was in the area. Now they had to be more stealthy, and they were in a hurry to leave the area before they were found out.

Crossing a swamp that same day, Two Crow's sled went through the ice where beaver had kept a channel. Two Crows was thoroughly soaked from the waist down, but there was no time to build a fire and dry out. They had to keep moving to avoid discovery by the other trapper. By the time they rested, Two Crows' feet were badly frozen. He knew how serious a matter it was, but he also knew they had to continue. Gradually the aching in his feet faded and they became numb.

That night, Two Crows sat by the fire contemplating the turn of events, and what it probably meant for him. His feet had quit aching some time ago, and now had no feeling in them at all, as if they belonged to someone else. LaBeque's silence was not reassuring, and when he looked at Two Crows, the half-breed felt cold in a different way. He realized he would be a burden to LaBeque, and he knew LaBeque didn't like to be burdened. He also knew the profits would be greater if they didn't have to be divided.

That night the northwest wind picked up and the wolves howled around them in the bitter cold while LaBeque slept. But Two Crows was too restless and worried to sleep, and he couldn't get warm. He was awake and heard the wolves when they came into their camp. He yelled at them, but couldn't stand on his frozen legs to chase them off. The frightened dogs whined and barked pitifully. They wanted to run for it, which would have been disaster for both men. The commotion woke

LaBeque who rose quickly, grabbed his rifle and fired a shot at the wolves. The loud crack was nearly too much for the frightened dogs, and they would all have run off if they hadn't been left in their traces. Two dogs did manage to get away, and were not seen again. It took LaBeque over an hour to untangle the dogs in their traces.

Two Crows had been crawling about on his hands and knees during the rucus because he couldn't stand. When things settled, he slowly rolled around to see LaBeque standing at the edge of the fire light, staring silently at him. They returned to their bed rolls, but Two Crows didn't sleep the rest of the night.

The next day, Two Crows seemed a bit hopeful when LaBeque didn't harness up the team and leave him to die in the snow. He pulled off his mukluks and found his feet were an odd waxy color, and felt hard. The two men spent most of the day skinning and bundling pelts, but with little conversation. Later, LaBeque got up without a word and shot one of the dogs that had gone lame. "We need fresh meat," he said while skinning it by the fire. That was when Two Crows knew it was the end of the trail for him. LaBeque had only enough dogs to pull one sled now. If it was between him and the furs, Two Crows knew what LaBeque would be carrying out on his sled. They ate the dog in silence.

Snow was falling heavily the next morning, and Two Crows watched as LaBeque packed his sled with as many furs as he could possibly carry. LaBeque announced he was leaving, and sounded almost sincere thanking Two Crows for his help. He told him he had never planned to share the profits, and that recent events had simply made their "inevitable parting" come sooner than he'd expected.

Reclining on his bed roll against the trunk of a fallen

tree, Two Crows said nothing and expressed no emotion in response. They both knew he couldn't walk on his frozen legs, and left alone was doomed to freeze to death in the snow. Before leaving, LaBeque pulled a half-empty bottle of rum from his sled and tossed it to Two Crows. Then, impatient to get away, he cracked his whip over the dogs and heaved the heavy sled into motion.

The team struggled across a small swamp and faded from view in the trees. LaBeque's shouts and the yelping of dogs soon faded too, and the forest became absolutely silent. Two Crows mumbled something in Cree as he sat with the bottle of liquor and watched the snow fall.

Later that day, LaBeque's progress was slowed by the death in the harness of one of the older dogs, whose poor heart just burst from the strain of the sled. LaBeque made camp for the night on the spot.

While he ate the dog by his fire, LaBeque considered his predicament and for the first time began to worry. He decided to alter his route and travel an easier way along a river. It was the only way, with the dogs getting weaker.

The next morning, LaBeque forced the dogs on until they came to the frozen river. There they found the snow was packed harder and the going was easier. They began to make better time again, but still not fast enough. LaBeque now only wanted to get out of the woods with his furs as fast as he could. He began to take chances.

He also began seeing strange footprints in the snow. He knew well the tracks of every animal in the woods, and read their sign as casually as a newspaper. All the tracks looked normal, except they seemed to be made by three-legged animals. One day he saw a fisher watching him from the trees a short distance away. It startled him as it ran off at an awkward gait on three legs. That was the first one. Later he saw mink and otter, all crippled in some way, and yet able to run at amazing speeds with their crippled lurching. They were disgusting to him. He began avoiding the trees along the river banks where they seemed to be.

That reckless avoidance cost LaBeque dearly. He got too close to thin ice near a rapids, and the team broke through. The lead dog went through first, got caught in the current and was swept beneath the ice. The ice gave under the next dogs, but LaBeque risked his life to cut the traces before the sled followed. Only two of the exhausted, emaciated dogs survived the catastrophe. The sled and furs were saved but there was no way those last two dogs could pull the load. LaBeque cursed his luck. He lightened the load and with great effort managed to get the sled to the bank to a sheltered spot, then retrieved the rest of the furs. It was early, but all he could do was set up camp. LaBeque needed to think.

This area of the country must be heavily trapped, LaBeque figured as he boiled water over his fire. It seemed like every furry creature he saw must have been in a trap at one time or another. So many cripples and three-legged animals. They gave him the willies for some reason. It occurred to LaBeque that any trapper who let so many animals get away couldn't be too skilled or clever at trapping.

That was it! There was another trapper in the area! All LaBeque had to do was wait and watch for the inexperienced fool and trick him or eliminate him if need be. Then LaBeque could not only take the man's dogs, but collect his furs as well. It was so simple a plan that LaBeque chuckled to himself out loud. Suddenly he whirled and threw a piece of firewood at a red squirrel that was getting into the remains of his provisions. He missed, and the squirrel darted away. Damn, that little critter moved fast on three legs, thought LaBeque.

That night LaBeque slept peacefully, knowing all he had to do was wait for that fool trapper to return. In fact, he slept so peacefully that his last two dogs ran off in the night and deserted him. He should have tied them up, of course, but it wasn't important. Both of the dogs were three-legged cripples anyway, and wouldn't be any good at pulling a sled anymore.

With all his dogs gone, LaBeque could concentrate his efforts on searching for that trapper. He could hardly wait to find the fellow. His mind conjured up various lines of deceit to hand the fool as he ate the last of his beans for breakfast. No problem. That other trapper probably had a food cache not far away.

LaBeque went to his sled and unlashed his snowshoes from the sides. He checked his map and made a mental note of the area so he could be sure to find the place later. Then he set out down the river, the direction he thought he'd be most likely to meet the other trapper.

As he snowshoed away from his sled full of furs, he noticed the crippled creatures following him at a distance. The miserable wretches, thought LaBeque. He hated them, but he sure wished he had their pelts on his sled. Their persistent presence was becoming more unnerving than annoying. Maybe if he ignored them, they'd go away and get trapped again.

Within an hour, LaBeque did come across the trail of the other trapper. Who would have thought it would be so easy? Who would have thought another trapper would be working territory this far away from everyone else? Now all LaBeque had to do was wait until the man came along to check his traps, and walked into...he laughed out loud at the thought of trapping a trapper, the ultimate catch.

Curiosity was a weakness with LaBeque though, and he decided to follow the man's trail. Maybe he'd gain some advantage by understanding his methods.

As he snowshoed the trail, he noted these were fertile grounds for trapping. There seemed to be fur-bearing animals everywhere, the pesky little beggars. They were really getting on LaBeque's nerves too. Everywhere he looked there seemed to be another one hobbling for cover behind a clump of brush or uprooted tree. The snow was covered by their three-legged tracks. How LaBeque hated them. They all should have been dead, caught by this inept fool's traps.

Who was this trapper anyway? Usually a man marked his traps so he could identify them. There was a familiar trap site ahead on the river bank and LaBeque decided he'd check the trap to see who it belonged to. He pulled off his snow shoes and plowed through soft, hip-deep snow to the river's edge. Everything looked all right, as LaBeque studied the scene. After digging around and breaking some ice, he pulled up a trap with a mink's foot still in it. For some reason it made his skin crawl, though he'd seen it many times. Ignoring the foot, LaBeque examined the trap and found a mark scratched into the steel.

The trap dropped from his hand as though it were red hot, and disappeared in the deep snow at his feet. LaBeque was stunned, confused.

Stepping backward away from the trap site, he almost tripped in the deep snow. He nervously looked around, feeling he was being watched. He needed to get away from there.

He struggled up the bank to get his snowshoes and a damned three-legged martin was gnawing at their rawhide lacing. LaBeque shouted a curse and lunged at the animal. As he did, the snow around his left leg heaved and exploded in the air around him with a muffled metallic sound. LaBeque was stopped so abruptly he fell headlong in the deep snow. As he fell he heard the sound of his leg bones breaking and searing pain burst in arcs from all his extremities. His face was buried in the snow which muffled his screams.

The cold snow on his face robbed him of the merciful relief of unconsciousness. He desperately needed to see what had happened, but couldn't move for the searing pain in his left leg. Neither could he stay lying face first in the snow gasping for air. Gradually he became aware that his right leg was OK, his arms, everything else was OK. But his left leg somewhere below the knee... LaBeque braced and pushed himself to kneel dizzily on his good right leg to see what the problem was. When he saw, he fainted dead away from pain and horror.

When he had lunged at the martin, he had stepped right into a bear trap. The huge steel jaws with two inch teeth had slammed together, nearly severing his left leg in their terrible bite. The cruel teeth went through his fur-lined leather mukluks, through layers of wool, through muscle and bone.

Eventually the cold or the pain brought LaBeque around again. He tried to move, but everything he did caused pain. Slowly, with agonizing effort he worked himself around so he could sit up in the snow and look at his leg. The trap was heavy, probably 70 or 80 pounds. He placed his hands on the jaws, clenched his teeth, and put every ounce of desperate strength he had into spreading the trap open. The jaws would not relent. Bracing against a small tree he worked himself up to stand on the spring, hoping all his weight would relieve the pressure. The jaws not only didn't move, he fell in the snow and passed out again from new explosions of pain. Coming to, he felt cold, and his leg seemed numb below the trap.

As he lay in the bloodied snow, he noticed in horror around him the furry forest creatures, staring with their black little eyes. LaBeque's blood chilled in his veins, and he shuddered. He felt a tree branch on the ground under him and feverishly dug it out of the snow. As he screamed curses and brandished the stick at the creatures, they retreated, but LaBeque knew they'd be back. They'd always be back. They'd never leave him alone.

Well, they weren't going to get him. Not Jaque LaBeque. He knew he was in bad shape, and he'd die there for sure if he didn't get out of that trap. He felt around his waist and found his skinning knife. Pulling it out, he looked at the animals and then at his leg in the trap. The bone was badly broken and the leg numb below the trap, so the decision was easier. He broke off a stick and put it between his teeth, then went to work with the knife.

It was easier to do than he thought it would be. The pain wasn't as bad as the trap had been. He used strips of his pant leg to tie-off the stump, and the cold helped stop the blood. Afraid to rest just yet, he built a fire.

Darkness was coming on, and LaBeque hobbled around gathering firewood from a nearby deadfall. He was weak, but determined. As he sat by the fire with his throbbing stump, he thought about his predicament. He cursed his luck and he cursed Two Crows. Above all, he cursed the three-legged furry creatures that stared at him from the fringe of the firelight which flickered in their eyes.

LaBeque propped himself up and tried to think about what he needed to do. His concentration wavered between dream and reality with the waves of pain from his leg. He was no longer sure what reality was. He wasn't even sure what had brought him to this predicament.

One thought finally rose to the surface of his consciousness, and that was that he was probably going to die out there in the woods. Those hateful little animals would get him and pick his bones.

With that thought, LaBeque let out a shriek and lunged wildly at the growing throng of little animals around him. That brought on more pain, but they lurched awkwardly back on crippled limbs. LaBeque knew he'd have to feed the fire through the night to keep them away. He used his knife again to cut a sapling for a crutch and a weapon. Then hobbling around like one of the creatures he detested, he gathered more wood. With the last of his strength, he brushed the snow off himself as best he could to avoid getting wet. Cold, exhausted, alone and crippled, LaBeque settled back against a tree by his little fire. He was drowsy, but resisted sleep, fearing he'd never wake up. His eyes closed for a moment, then he jerked awake again. Through the smoke of the fire he could make out Two Crows sitting across from him, grinning in silence. How could Two Crows have gotten there? That devil must have tricked him, and then followed after to kill him. LaBeque cursed him, but the half-breed just sat grinning in silence, looking as he had when LaBeque left him. It was like a dream.

And he did dream. LaBeque dreamed of the animals attacking him and tearing at his flesh, and he awoke screaming and thrashing. The fire was nearly out and his body was shaking so much from cold and fear it took all his concentration to coax the embers back to life. When the flames flickered high again, LaBeque looked around. No sign of Two Crows, but hundreds of pairs of little red eyes reflected the firelight as they stared at him from the surrounding darkness.

With all his determination, LaBeque resolved to survive

the night. He'd start hiking out in the morning if he could. If only those creatures would leave him alone. He was so cold, so tired.

And maybe that's just what LaBeque did. No one knows for sure.

Some weeks later, trappers found the frozen body of Two Crows just as LaBeque had left him. His icy hand still held a half-full bottle of rum, and his face still wore its grimacing grin. Later, after spring thaw, others found LaBeque's sled where he'd left it, piled high with rotting furs. Still later that summer, two men canoeing a river in the area found a bear trap on the bank with the grizzly remains of a man's leg, clad in a mukluk, still clamped in the jaws. There was never found, however, any remains of the trapper Jaque LaBeque.

The Lake With No Name

A map of the Boundary Waters area gives one a sense of an almost endless number of lakes and waterways. Bodies of water in various shapes and sizes dot the area like beads of water on canvas. There seems to be as much water as there is dry land, and that's what makes the character of this great wilderness so unique. For the most part, only the bodies of water have been given names, which still is perhaps the most simple means of telling where one is in relation to the rest of the area. Before humans traveled this interlaced network of waterways, there were no names.

How these lakes got their names could be an interesting study in itself. Many still retain their Indian names, or perhaps an English translation. Many lakes were named by explorers and others by early surveyors. Some were given names by the old loggers who worked much of this land in the early part of the century. The variety of names given to identify these irregular blue spots on the map seems to have taxed the imaginations of those who needed to account for them all. Eventually they must have given up.

If the map is a good one, the kind that shows the detail needed for navigation, one sees something else. There are still a lot of them left unnamed. They're the smaller lakes that are "off the beaten path." One of those small, unnamed lakes is the subject of this story.

Those who passed this story down are long gone now, but even they didn't seem to know for certain where this lake is. Supposedly, it was found by a survey team around the turn of the last century. At least, that's the first actual white man's account of it. Before that, there were only a few obscure voyageur tales and ancient Indian legends that briefly mentioned the existence of this one, special lake.

According to some unfinished and sketchy old survey reports, it could be only a pond of about fourteen acres, maybe sixteen, but small to be sure. It has no streams flowing in or out. There are no portages going to or from the lake, at least none that have been maintained in modern times.

It looks like any other lake in the area, with rocky shores and a stockade of dense pine and birch all around. Old word-of-mouth descriptions have noted however, that there are some subtle differences about the lake which an astute observer might notice.

That astute wilderness traveler might observe when coming to this lake that there are no shore weeds growing from the water, no lily pads or cattails. It appears to be very deep, judging by the darkness of the water. There won't be any signs of muskrat or beaver houses along the shore, no loons or gulls trolling the surface. No fish.

It's dead calm. Always. Perhaps that's because the lake is small, and protected by that barrier of tall dark pines around it. But these are the subtle things which only a careful observer might notice upon coming to this lake. The big difference is that on this lake, nothing floats. Nothing at all.

There are only a few vague accounts of the lake, mostly murky legends. The most lucid one happened about 100 years ago, but don't bother trying to verify it.

It seems a man stumbled out of the woods one day into a mining camp near the south of what is now the

Boundary Waters Canoe Area. He was in bad shape, suffering from malnutrition, fever from infections, exhaustion, exposure to biting insects and the elements. The man had traveled for many days, maybe several weeks, cross country through the woods with only the clothes on his back. No map, no compass, no equipment of any kind. His clothes were shredded from the trek, and apparently so was his mental state.

The camp clerk, who took care of the medical needs of the men, put him to bed to be nursed back to health. During his recovery the man ranted about a lake, but no one paid much attention, figuring him to be delirious from the fever.

After several days, the man seemed recovered, and insisted he had to get back to Duluth with his story. The camp clerk felt he was not strong enough to travel, and being curious, they asked him to stay and share his story.

The man told the clerk he had been with a team sent into the woods to survey and upgrade maps of the area for potential logging and mining exploration. A three-man team, they had been traveling for several weeks by canoe over land and water, surveying as they went. Living off the land, one of the men hunted, while the other two did the surveying work.

They were pretty well established in their routine, and although the work was hard, and bugs and rugged terrain made the job miserable at times, they were making good progress. The man went on, and became more and more upset, eventually began ranting again as he had during his fever. After a couple shots of medicinal whisky to settle him down, he continued.

It seemed so routine. Their survey brought them to a lake just like all the others they'd crossed. It was his turn to stay on the shore with the surveying transom while the other two men paddled across the little lake with their gear. He would then "sight" the stake they would set up on the other side and record the data before they paddled back across to pick him up and continue on.

But as they paddled, the canoe rode lower and lower, until his partners realized they were sinking. He could hear the urgency in their voices as they started to head back. They weren't that far out, he thought, they'd come right back and patch a leak or something. He laughed as he called out to them, saying that they needed a bath anyway.

Suddenly, the canoe slipped under with all their gear. Everything sank out of sight immediately. His partners were both strong swimmers, he knew, because they had all been forced to swim in rapids when their canoe had overturned on past occasions. A hand thrashed out for an instant – grasping – then was gone. Even their paddles.

He watched in stunned silence. Desperate logic told him his partners had dived to recover the equipment. He waited. They didn't surface. The lake was glassy calm again. Nothing floated to the surface to suggest that there had just been a canoe with two men and all their equipment out there.

Then the realization that they needed help brought him back to his senses. Maybe they were tangled in the equipment and pulled down. He jumped into the lake to help them.

As soon as he hit the water he realized something was horribly wrong. He sank like a stone. Deep. He swam and kicked, but the only direction he went was down. It was dark, and the water was cold. Very cold. He pulled hard for the surface, but kept sinking. No current, no suction, just no buoyancy. His flailing hand touched an underwater rock outcropping, part of the ledge at the shore he had just been standing on. He caught it and began pulling himself upward towards the light of the sky above the surface. His lungs were about to burst. He was beginning to inhale water when he finally broke the surface, coughing and gagging.

Panic had him fighting for his life, and he struggled with his last energy to free himself from the water. After clawing his way back onto land he lay coughing and retching until passing out.

He didn't know how long he lay there, but eventually he regained his senses and some of his strength. A raft, he thought, a log, something. He went into the woods, found some dry dead logs and dragged them to the lake. Not willing to step into the deep water again, he put the logs in first, hoping to use them as floatation. They sank immediately. So did other logs. He threw dry sticks after them, and they sank in the same manner. He dropped to his knees in frustration, staring at the lake. It was quiet. A dry leaf fluttered down lightly through the air and landed on the surface of the water before him. It disappeared without hesitation into the depths.

He didn't recall much after that. Confused and in shock, he hung around the lake several days to see if any of their gear would maybe wash ashore so he could recover it. It didn't.

Without any equipment or supplies, he soon resorted to eating berries and anything else that looked edible. The fourth morning, the sound of brush being forced aside near the shore of the lake awakened him. It was a moose about 30 yards away. The big animal walked down to the water, no doubt hoping to escape the flies. It waded into the shallows, then deeper, and began to swim for the far shore. The man sat up abruptly to watch. It didn't get far. The powerful beast struggled desperately for only a moment before going under. It didn't come back up.

After that, the man got up and started walking in the direction he best recalled being south.

The man left the logging camp shortly after telling his tale, and eventually made his way to Duluth. After giving his wild account of what had happened, he spent some time in jail. No one was willing to believe his wild tale. His partners never showed up, and fowl play was suspected, but without evidence to convict him of any crime, he was released. All the records of the location of the lake went down with the canoe of course so further investigation was not possible.

As for the man, his reputation was ruined and no one would hire him. He was a shady character, and thought to be crazy. People who knew of the incident believed he had something to do with the disappearance of his partners. He wandered the streets and turned to liquor. He told his story to anyone who would buy him a bottle at first, or just a drink later. He tried working at odd jobs, but nothing around water. Seems he developed an irrational fear of water. He never got in a canoe or boat of any kind again, and didn't care to watch others set out in one either. Eventually he even quit bathing, and became reclusive. No one knows if he died or moved away, but eventually he was just gone. The lake, wherever it is, supposedly remains.

Deacon's Bench Tales

Lumberjacks have provided a rich lore of stories that often started during evening sessions in the north woods bunk houses, just before lights out. Most bunk houses were hard up for any kind of furniture, but they usually had a bench of sorts where a few of the men could sit and relax by the warmth of the wood stove. It might have been an acquired piece of actual furniture in some cases, or sometimes the bench may have been made of rough lumber. Maybe the bench was just crudely shaped logs split or hewn enough to provide a surface to sit on. This small concession to comfort was usually called the "deaco bench," probably due to the amount of "testifying" that was done by some who sat on it. This was where many of the heroes and tall tales of logging camps originated. Truth and fiction were often merged, and over time it became hard to know what was real and what wasn't. Occasionally there were stories of events or characters which were more incredible than those which were made up.

Olaf Sandvik was a young man when he immigrated to this country sometime after the turn of the last century. Like many men who emigrated to the area at that time, he found work in the logging camps of northern Minnesota. Olaf was a likable guy, easy going to the point of being submissive. A good thing too, because Olaf was big. Not only big, but powerfully built with the strength that comes from a life of working as a beast of burden. He was a strong man among strong men. But even as some of his kinder friends pointed out behind his back, his thickest muscle was the one between his ears. Olaf himself put it best when in his thick measured accent he said, "Ja, ay may not be tu smart, but ay can lift heafy 'tings." That statement, along with his size, was good enough to land him his first job in a logging camp.

Olaf was a simple man, short on schooling and not too sure how to use what little education he had. This, as well as his size and strength, made him the brunt of a lot of practical jokes around the logging camp. Fortunately, he took it all in stride, and could even see the humor in a predicament that would leave him shaking his head and, with a sheepish grin just saying "uffda." Sometimes the jokes backfired however, and left the jokers with nothing to do but pick up their jaws and walk away.

Like the time a leaky water barrel had sat outside and froze to the ground. Nobody could move it. Thinking they'd have a little fun with Olaf, they pulled a horse-drawn work sleigh along side the barrel as though they intended to load it aboard. Someone got Olaf to come help, knowing that the barrel wouldn't budge. Normally it took two good men to lift that big barrel of water and place it on the sleigh, even if it wasn't frozen to the ground. But they didn't tell Olaf that. He put his arms around the barrel and strained and heaved while the others smirked and winked at each other. Then with a groaning, cracking sound the barrel broke free and he set it on the sleigh.

Flapjacks

It takes a lot to feed a man as strong as Olaf, and Olaf was a prodigious eater. Most loggers were. But before anyone would notice, a man really had to pack away the chow. Such a man was Big Ivan, who worked – and ate – at a rival logging camp not far away. It was said he ate all winter as though he didn't expect to see food during the off-season. Big Ivan didn't brag about his appetite… he didn't need to. His friends bragged for him. All Big Ivan did was smile and pat his considerable girth.

Well, word of Big Ivan's capacity to consume soon traveled to the camp where Olaf worked. To Olaf's pals, it sounded like a challenge, and they were always willing to put their friend to the test, especially if they felt sure they could profit by some crafty wagering. After the customary confrontational boasting over which camp had the biggest chow hound, a contest was arranged between Big Ivan and Olaf. Since flapjacks were a mainstay in the diet at every logging camp, flapjacks were the entrée that would determine which camp had bragging rights. That Sunday, everybody's day off, it would be flapjacks at high noon.

Olaf loved pancakes. Of course, so did Big Ivan. A cookee from Ivan's camp volunteered to keep "em comin" as long as one man or the other was still able to chew. When the moment of truth arrived, the betting was heavy on both sides. Olaf and Ivan started off with an equal stack of six plate-sized flapjacks, covered with butter and syrup. Ivan plowed through this first plateful to take an early lead, but had to wait for the next serving to finish cooking, and Olaf caught up. Both men kept packing in the cakes while their respective fans shouted encouragement and taunted the other side. Soon they were neck-and-neck at two dozen with no sign of slowing. Then, on the 27th flapjack, Big Ivan paused to inhale and sigh. His managers were on him instantly, massaging his bulging belly and stroking his throat muscles. He rolled his glazing eyes and valiantly ordered another stack, but Olaf had pulled ahead.

The score was Olaf 32 – Big Ivan 28, and the intensity of the competition caused the men on both sides to grow quiet so the contestants could concentrate. In grim determination, Ivan lifted another forkful of pancake, as the faint sound of a bell pealed in the distance.

Suddenly, Olaf stood up. Emitting a huge belch that sounded like a bull moose in rut, he wiped syrup from his mouth with his sleeve and stated flatly that he had to go. He had just heard the dinner bell back at camp and the cook didn't tolerate anyone being late for meals. Without another word Olaf walked away leaving a stunned gallery and Big Ivan gagging on number 29.

Of Lice and Men

Sanitation and cleanliness were not a high priority in the bunk houses in the old logging camps. With the lack of bathing or laundry facilities and sleeping on straw-padded bunks, body lice were practically inevitable. The close quarters of the bunk house meant it usually didn't take long before an entire crew would be infested. This was not an uncommon occurrence at logging camps, and many men became all too familiar with the intimate little insects and the condition of being "lousy."

To deal with the problem, periodic de-lousing parties were held. Men would bathe and their clothes were boiled, producing some limited, if temporary, relief from the lice. But these hardy lumberjacks made the best of a sensitive situation, and that occasionally led to bragging about the number or size of the lice that infested one's person.

Olaf was not to be out-loused. He claimed to host a pure-bred strain of hardy Nordic stock that came over on the boat from the old country with him. These were prolific beauties that carried themselves with pride, and if you were bitten by one, you knew it was, well – a kind of special experience. When de-lousing times came around, Olaf was always careful to save a good breeding pair to preserve the blood lines.

With the bragging, of course, came challenges and betting. One midwinter a newcomer had been listening to the regular jawing at the deacon's bench. The boys were topping each other with one yarn after the other, each lie getting more incredible than the last. Charlie, the new man, had heard enough and decided to jump into the competition with a topper of his own. The boys got kind of quiet though, when Charlie chose to brag about his lice.

He went on and on about them, how big they were and how mean they could bite. He maintained these weren't just any lice. He'd got them from a bear he'd helped skin that fall, and that's where they'd gotten all their lousy attributes. They were by far the most ornery, irascible, irritating infestation he'd ever had to put up with, and a lesser man couldn't survive the torment.

Well, the boys allowed as how he might be right about his lice being too much for them, but they assured him Olaf's hybrids were about as bad as bad can get. That amounted to a challenge. After a bit of contentious posturing, normal in these situations, a contest was proposed to settle the matter.

One evening before lights out – those who were interested – and that happened to be a majority, were gathered around the glowing wood stove. A kerosene lamp was placed down low, illuminating a close-pressed arena of grisly, whiskered faces crowded together just off the bunk house floor. Jostling close behind them in rising tiers were other glowing faces, and hands full of currency exchanging side bets. On the rough floor boards a charcoal ring had been crudely drawn with a burnt piece of wood.

Charlie, on his knees before the ring, reached deep into his long underwear to select a contestant. He replaced several before choosing his champion louse. Olaf was more prepared, and looked impressive if a bit theatrical when he produced a snoose can. On releasing the insect from its confinement, he muttered something about the empty can having been half-full when he had put the vicious little pest inside.

Each man looked rather comical as he delicately handled the insects with thick, callused fingers more accustomed to gripping heavy tool handles. But amusing appearances did not belie the serious nature of the event, especially with the money riding on either side. The bunk house was quiet, except for the crackling hiss of the wood stove.

Charlie shook the tenacious bug from his thumb as it seemed reluctant to be evicted from warmer quarters. The louse landed in the ring in an apparently foul mood, and immediately began pacing around looking for something – or someone – to sink its formidable jaws into. The men winced in unison out of respect.

Olaf, in contrast, simply placed his thumb inside the ring. The huge louse dismounted with the air of a European aristocrat, drawing a chorus of admiring expletives from the crowd.

The two lice were aware of each other almost immediately. They began circling one another looking for an opening, while protecting themselves from the other's vicious attack. It was as if there was a need to jealously protect the territory of their respective hosts. It was a primeval competition between the two bugs, beyond the understanding of humans. You could have heard an eye blink in the gallery, if anyone would have dared.

Then, the two lice stopped circling each other. Facing each other they began bobbing up and down. Suddenly, they locked forearms/legs or whatever, and together they leaped into the closest bunch of whiskers available, and buried themselves deep. Those whiskers adorned Olaf's face, as he had been watching the contest from just inches off the floor.

Olaf jerked back with his eyes big and round. Everybody else jerked back staring at Olaf. He leaned forward and tried brushing the little buggers from his beard, but they weren't coming out. Somebody said "give him a comb!" but no one had one handy. Others started pawing through Olaf's whiskers, which could have led to a migration, but all was to no avail. The two lice had made a getaway in the huddled mass of men in that dark bunk house.

There was a lot of grumbling as all bets were now off and money was returned all around. Olaf went to bed, but he didn't sleep well. He felt kind of creepy-crawly and couldn't get comfortable.

But that was just the beginning. It was generally accepted later, that the lice were a male and female pair, because it wasn't long before the whole camp was infested with a terrible outbreak of the most ornery, irascible, irritating infestation of lice ever to plague the North Woods.

Snoose to Snooze

When winter closed in around the camp, the nights got long and men were ready to get their much needed rest after a long day. But in Olaf's bunk house, sleep was hard to come by. Olaf snored, as only Olaf could – long and loud. Olaf felt bad about his snoring, but couldn't help it. When he'd fall into a deep sleep, his snoring was enough to wake hibernating animals and send them looking for quieter territory.

Olaf's tremendous snoring sometimes drew air back down the stove pipes, reversing the draft on the fires and filling the bunkhouse with smoke. The fires smoldered giving off little heat on those minus-forty-degree nights, and men coughed and shivered in the cold smoky bunk house, getting little rest. They were tired in the morning and not able to work hard enough during the day. Something had to be done.

Some of the men thought that if they could just get to

sleep before Olaf started snoring, they would sleep alright. Since Olaf enjoyed a good cup of coffee, they had the cook brew up a pot full in the evenings. He made it extra strong for Olaf, in hopes of keeping him awake long enough so others could get to sleep first. But Olaf refused to drink coffee after dinner, claiming it kept him awake.

Then someone had a bright idea. They started collecting the soggy, used coffee grounds from the coffee pot and putting it in Olaf's snoose can. Just as a joke at first, but Olaf didn't seem to notice or mind. In fact, he seemed to like it, even better than snoose without coffee. Soon he started using coffee grounds for snoose on a regular basis. At night he was accustomed to packing in a mouthful at bed time. That did the trick. With his mouth full of coffee ground "snoose," Olaf got enough caffeine from the coffee grounds to keep him awake longer, and prevent him from falling into a deep, snoring sleep. The men could get a head start at falling asleep before Olaf, so they got a full night's rest.

After that, the fires in the stove drew normally and kept the bunkhouse cozy without smoking-up the place. The men slept soundly and were rested for the next work day. Even the wildlife were grateful, as the woods at night were peaceful again.

Whiskers

The topic had turned to beards – chin-whiskers – as several of us regulars waited out the rain over refills of "bottom-of-the-pot" coffee in our booth at Fran's cafe. We'd been talking about the 100-year anniversary of our little northeastern Minnesota town, and the various events to celebrate the occasion. One part involved local men avoiding the razor for the summer – as if men around here need a reason not to shave. But it was to be a beard contest, and those men who didn't grow whiskers would be "fined", or "thrown in jail."

Anyway, as we were talking beards, ol' Milo Velacek appeared in the door of the cafe, looking around to check out who was inside. After noting the company, he parked his dog outside the door and walked up to the counter. That's the way he was, cautious around people. Milo had learned years ago to choose his company, as he had long been the subject of unflattering rumors and rude comments about his state of mind or some odd behavior. Slapping rain from his old felt hat, he perched his lanky frame on a stool alone.

Everybody around here knows Milo, though no one would recognize his face. As long as anyone can remember, it's been hidden behind the longest, thickest growth of facial hair on the Range. Not everyone appreciates beards, but even those who don't are impressed by the density and texture of Milo's. From just behind the corner of his eyes, angling to his nostrils, a cascade of lush, regal whiskers – now more salt than pepper – reaches to the top of his bib overalls. At our booth, his arrival stifled the beard conversation, and our silent awe paid homage to the male hormone.

Milo, a bachelor about 60 years old, preferred the company of animals and normally didn't talk much to people. Not that he was unfriendly; he was just quiet and kept to his own affairs. Maybe shy would be a better word for it, but shy to the point of being unsociable by local standards. He wasn't unlikable though, just different.

If you scrape enough of the crust off some people, you often find something interesting underneath. With Milo, it was his affinity for animals. It started with his dog, a fat, smelly old mutt named Moses (because he found him by the bullrushes in a ditch when he was a pup). Moses had thick, matted black hair all over except around the muzzle where he'd gone gray. Totally devoted to each other, Moses waddled at Milo's side everywhere they went.

They didn't come into town often, but over the years Milo had gotten to know most everybody, and of course we all knew him – and Moses. But only a few got to know much about him that was not based on hearsay. Oh there were plenty of stories about Milo feeding the deer, Milo and his birds, Milo patching up an injured creature of some sort. But Art Rekola had one of the best stories.

Art talked Milo into taking him to one of his favorite fishing spots once. At their campsite that evening, a big old bear came out of the brush looking for something to eat. Milo fed him their day's catch as Art looked on from a distance. While the bear ate their fish, Milo pulled ticks off the bear's rear end, just above its tail. Each tick he pulled, he tossed to the bear and the bear ate it. When it was done eating the fish, the bear walked off into the woods. Art said that was enough for him; he was leaving before the bear came back. Milo told Art not to worry, the bear would not be back. When Art asked Milo "what the hell made him think that," Milo gave him a strange glance and said the bear "felt uncomfortable" with Art around. Whatever the case, the bear did not come back while they were camped there.

It got so that when people had a sick pet or farm animal, they'd ask Milo's advice or help. He was no veterinarian, but had taught himself a lot about healing plants and herbs, and he had an uncommon common sense in dealing with all sorts of creatures. For all his lack of social skills, his extraordinary way with animals had gained Milo a reputation, even if it established him as a local oddity.

Back in our booth, as we talked of how he'd managed to hide behind such a prolific set of whiskers for so long, it occurred to Carl, who's lived here all his life, that he'd never seen ol' man Velacek without that beard. He called over to Milo, asking him, "how long had it been since he'd seen his own face."

The rest of us thought that was a bit bold, but a fair question. Of course it wasn't like he opened up right away and started explaining what motivated him to grow his crop of whiskers, but it got Velacek talking. At first he turned on his stool and eyed us suspiciously without reply. We assured him we were genuinely interested, not wanting to trouble him. We were all in fact considering growing beards for the town centennial.

Perhaps he felt that he was about to be taken seriously, and his beard was something about himself that, in our company, he could safely share. Perhaps he was just in a rare talkative mood. We weren't at all prepared for the story that was ol' man Velacek's answer.

He began feeling us out, offering a few details to judge our response. After a pause, Milo offered that he, "wasn't born with it, ya know". Some of us remained unconvinced. Maybe it was just because there was nothing better to do on a rainy day, maybe we were just bored, but we soon found ourselves wrapped up in his tale.

"I didn't have a beard when I was young, and that's getting to be awhile back now. But I got this beard when I was young, and I haven't seen what I look like under it since then. I didn't grow it for my health or vanity, or to save on razors. I didn't grow it to hide behind either. Oh, there's times when I'm tempted to shave it off just to have a look, and other times I'd like to shave it off because it's hot or just a nuisance. But I can't. It isn't that I might not like what I see under these whiskers, mind you. I gave up on how I looked years ago. It's just that I...well I can't shave this beard. I just don't want to...forget.

"Now I suppose that wants an explanation, but after all these years all I've got is this story. You won't believe it, and I can't blame you if you don't. I've lived with it over half my life, and I'm not getting any younger. It won't make any difference to me what you think."

At this point, the man was talking like he needed to unburden himself, and the sincerity of Velacek's words had our attention. But it was the look in his eyes that truly held us when he spoke.

"When I was young there was a rough period in my life when everything just went wrong. I was working in Chicago at a pretty good job making great money; had a nice place to live and a bright future. I met a young lady who was everything a man could hope for, and I guess we fell for each other, or so I thought. Everything was going right for me, but I felt something was missing and never could figure out what it was.

"I had a high-pressure job that demanded a huge time commitment. Being ambitious and well paid, I did my best and gave my heart and soul to the company. Eventually, I no longer had time for the young lady, and she left me for someone who paid attention to her.

"I replaced her with things that I could buy. But I had no time for them either, since my job wanted more and more of my life. The friends I had moved on with their lives, and I found another 'friend' in a bottle. I started drinking, sometimes heavily. I'm not sure whether it was my drinking or problems with the company, but I lost my job. I didn't lose my 'friend' though. In fact, I became closer to my 'friend' in the bottle, and it started running my schedule. I found myself available whenever my 'friend' was.

"I started hanging around with a rough crowd, and was stupid enough to cheat a few of them out of a bit of cash. It was more important for these guys to get even than to get their money back, and that meant my health was in serious jeopardy. It seemed like a good idea to become scarce for awhile, and that's what brought me to this North Country.

"I'd been to the border lakes on canoe trips when I was young, so I wasn't a complete stranger to the area and knew something about traveling by canoe. How I used to enjoy that country. It was a good place to run and hide, and the time seemed right time for an extended trip.

"But the lake country isn't a good place to escape what's in your heart. I'd come to avoid the angry goons I'd offended, but couldn't escape the turmoil that my life had become; and paddling wasn't bringing the peaceful refuge I sought.

"Then one day after crossing a portage, I set out on a big lake – don't even recall which one it was anymore. As I started to cross, dark clouds were moving in fast from the northwest toward the far end of the lake, and it looked like a good storm. The other side of the lake seemed like the best place to be, at least it would be out of the wind, so I started across. Not fast enough though. Bucking the headwind and whitecaps was wearing me out, and I knew I wasn't going to make it to the other side before the storm hit. When lightning flashed down the lake, I became concerned.

"A hundred yards off to my side was a tiny island – unexpected, and probably too small to show on my map. It did support a small, dense stand of black spruce, and I decided to take shelter there. Better to at least be on solid ground when the storm broke, I figured, than out in the middle of the lake in my canoe. The rain was moving down fast from the far end of the lake, so I pushed my tired arms harder, and pulled for the little island.

"I hauled the canoe safely up over the rocky shore and as I tied it to a tree, the first rain drops began spattering around me. I scrambled through a barrier of tag alder and into the spruce trees as the first heavy gusts of the storm rushed through their branches.

"Once through the tag alder I stumbled onto a path. I followed it to escape the storm, as it was easier going on the path than through the thick growth of the little island. I hurried down the path as thunder cracked over wind roaring through the tree tops, and big, cold drops of rain began pelting down.

"Soon I broke into a run, as though I might escape the storm that now assaulted the rocky shore of my island refuge. I was hurling myself down the rocky path as fast as I could go, not knowing why I ran or where I was going.

"I don't know how long I continued, but eventually I became winded and slowed to a brisk walking pace. My heart was pounding, my breathing was fast and heavy but I noticed it wasn't raining anymore. I noticed the wind had subsided too. At a normal walking pace, my senses gradually returned, but now seemed sharper, more intense. I started to think clearly again.

"Where was this path going, and why hadn't I reached its end yet? This was, after all, a tiny island. The path continued, but I stopped abruptly. Something wasn't right. On first reaching the island, I was sure it was so small I could have thrown a stone over it. After paddling to the lee side of the island to land the canoe, I was certain it was an island. But how could I have run so long on a path on a tiny island that shouldn't be large enough to even have a path, let alone one as long as this? And still, the path led on.

"I continued along the path, now wondering where it led. As I walked, the clouds parted and sunbeams probed through the treetops. The rain-washed air was so rich with the clean smell of pine-scented earth, it made me heady. The path led through lush forest, and the songs of birds and insects resumed with the sudden departure of the storm.

"I thought, 'enough of this, I should get back to my canoe. I've got a… I've got to be… well I just don't have time for this.' Hesitating on the path, I detected the faint sound of water, gurgling along in a stream somewhere nearby. It must flow to the lake, I reasoned, and I looked along the path for the stream.

"As I walked, the gurgling sound got louder, but I couldn't see any water through the dense undergrowth. The stream had to be small to be so hidden. Pausing again to listen for the stream, I now detected something else subtly mingled with its babbling sound. A voice, or maybe voices. The path was taking me to someone. I strained to hear where the talking was coming from and what was said, and the back of my neck got cold and prickly. The voice was calling me, personally. Not by my name, but… the voice knew me. It spoke intimately to my being. I felt it as much as heard it.

"I tell you it scared the daylights out of me. Once again I started running down the path in the opposite direction. I wanted to get back to my canoe and off that island as fast as I could. Fear of something unknown I guess, had a hold of me and I ran back down the path in the direction from which I'd come.

"In no time I realized it wasn't the same route I'd come on. I must have been running the wrong way. I turned around again and had the same feeling. Now my bearings were so mixed up I felt lost, yet I'd never left the path.

"There had been no forks in the trail, no side trips to distract me, and it seemed as if I'd been on the path for a mile, maybe two, or maybe... much longer. My heart was pounding, about to explode, and my head was ringing from anxiety. How could I get lost, never having left the path, on an island that was too small to have a path that went anywhere in the first place? I sat on a rock outcropping beside the path and put my head in my hands. 'Settle down Milo, you've got to keep your sense,' I said out loud to myself. 'Got to stay calm. It's just my imagination,' I reasoned. 'Sure could use a stiff drink right now.' I considered leaving the path and breaking through the woods to find the shore, but the thick brush was intimidating, and I realized that I'd get even more lost if I tried that. Sitting there waiting to collect my senses, the sound of the gurgling, babbling brook came to me through the trees, still calling to me.

"The voice had a calming effect as I sat there, even reassuring. If I confronted whoever it was, perhaps they could tell me which way to go to get back on track. When I resumed walking down the path following the sound of the brook and voices, a peaceful feeling came to me. I now felt I was going where I needed to be.

"The brook appeared beside the path, its clear rippling water hurrying along a fern-lined, stony bed. Meandering around boulders and through the roots of overhanging trees, it flowed to its ultimate destination. Following it a short distance, I reached its source – a small flowing spring. Mossy rocks and tree roots framed the little pool, and a blooming flower flashed a bright spot on its dark surface. The crystal clear water seeped up from the earthy depths in an endless, smooth and steady flow. I was thirsty.

"Kneeling beside the spring, I cupped my hand into the dark, cold, clear water and scooped up a drink. As I sucked the water from my palm, the rippling surface I'd disturbed rearranged my reflection into dancing shapes. The shimmering patterns of light now assumed the face of a beautiful young woman, and I blinked hard to test my vision. I was certain I was imagining or dreaming the vision, but could not take my eyes from her. I stared in silence, not wanting to disturb the water and spoil the illusion – if that's what it was. She smiled up at me and I heard her soft voice again in the gurgling of the brook.

"She spoke to me in realizations, saying that I had nothing to fear. I was aware, somehow, that she knew everything that had happened in my life – everything that I had done, everything that had mattered to me and everything that hadn't but should have. It was like seeing myself from a completely different perspective. I knew I didn't like where my life had been going, and I'd been running to escape the mess I'd made of it.

"She said that the only true treasures in life were already mine. They are the blessings the Creator has brought forth from the earth. Then she told me I could receive a new direction for my life in the form a gift which I could share with those who are not people.

"To receive the gift, all I needed to do was wash my face in the waters of the pool. The gift would be mine for the rest of my life, and included a personal reminder that would grow with my commitment to change.

"I wanted to change, to have a new direction in my life. I wanted that gift. I scooped from the pool and drenched my face with the refreshing water that washed my face clean, and with it my sense of being. I splashed more water on my face again and again, until even the front of my shirt was wet.

"The disturbance of the pool stirred up sediment, obliterating the vision and even my own reflection. But when I looked around me, the world seemed to have taken on a new beauty. I looked in the pool again, but she was not there. It didn't matter. For the first time in my life I felt at peace, and very tired. I lay back against a tree root and fell into a deep sleep.

"I don't know how long I slept, but it was enough to feel rested. When I awoke, the pool was still there, and the brook continued to babble and gurgle, but I heard no voice in its sound. By the sun it was late afternoon, and I vaguely remembered my canoe. I needed to find a place to camp. As I got to my feet, the feeling of peace and beauty was still with me, and I started walking on the path without anxiety or apprehension.

"I hadn't gone far before the sky became cloudy, and suddenly it started raining. I began to recognize something familiar about the path, but it looked somehow different. Changed. I liked it more now. The wet brush along the trail soaked my clothes, and in no time I came out of the tag alder onto the rocky shoreline of the lake.

"It had been quite a storm, but the rain had passed. Rolling thunder faded in the distance, and the waves on the shore – no longer driven by wind – became a dwindling, random chop.

"What had happened? My mind was a jumble not sure what was reality and what was a dream. I knew where I was now, but where had I been? I turned and looked back at the tag alder and the spruce beyond where I'd found the path. I started to go back, then stopped as something told me I couldn't. The path only went one direction. I had to move on; I couldn't stay there anymore. I was confused to the point of being dazed, but still there was that feeling of peace from within.

"The rain had stopped and off in the west I could see blue sky heading my way. I turned over my canoe and placed it in the calm waters on the lee side of the island. When I was putting my second pack in the canoe, I looked down into the water and saw someone's reflection looking back at me.

"I stumbled back on the rocks, shocked by what I'd seen. It was me! Cautiously I approached the water's edge to look at my reflection again.

"Sure I'd been out for nearly a week, but... in my reflection I watched my hand move slowly up to my face. I watched my fingers sink into the thick, dark beard that covered my features. It hadn't been there that morning. Stubble sure, I'd not shaved for a few days. But...

"Then her words resurfaced in my memory: '...a personal reminder would grow with my commitment to change,' I recalled.

"My hand clutched the whiskers and I gave a tug that made me wince. They were for real, but... how? How long had I been on this little island? Was this storm that just passed the same storm? How could that path have been so long on this small an island?

"Too many questions. Too strange. I wanted to get off that rock pile. I got in my canoe and shoved off, paddling hard to get away from – whatever that place, that island was. I paddled hard for the far shore, and not until I had made half the distance did I turn and look back.

"Sunlight illuminated the glowing trunks of birches and pines on the distant shore against the retreating dark storm. The high rock cliffs, still wet and shiny, were rich with deep earth colors, and sunlight sparkled off the glittering blue water. I heard birds singing and saw gulls floating on the breeze. Everything seemed more beautiful than it had appeared before, as though I saw it in a new light. But the island I did not see.

"It was gone. Disappeared, as if it had never been there. I referred to my map again and I turned the canoe for a better look, but the island was not on the map. It simply was not there anymore. I began to wonder if it ever had been, if maybe I was going crazy… I put my hand to my face and felt the full, thick beard which was still there, still reminded me.

"My gift was to be shared with those who are not people, and it has been a different direction for my life ever since. I've worn these whiskers as a reminder – and I've never forgotten."

Changeling

"**N**ow here's one for you," he said, tipping back his hat and leaning closer to add emphasis. "I was up northwest a'here on a fish'n trip with a bunch," he began, "and we figured we had the lake to ourselves. That's why we went there, y'know. Well, we'd been fish'n for a couple a days an' doin' pretty good too. Anyhow, one day we just figure'd we'd split up and try some different places on the lake. Me an' this other fella', we headed down along the shore line to this back bay that had a nice swampy area. He wanted to try for some bass in the snags."

I was with a group of guides hanging around back of an outfitter's place. Everyone was about finished putting away gear and hanging tents and packs to dry at the end of their trips. Activity was winding down and we were starting to relax, swapping stories about the "customers" they'd just spent the week with. There were always fish stories and amusing events or crazy things that happened on these trips, but this time the conversation had shifted toward the odd, inexplicable events that one occasionally sees in the wilderness.

"Anyhow," he continued, "we'd been drift'n around that bay and not hav'n any luck to speak of for quite awhile. We weren't pay'n much attention to things and floated pretty close to shore on one side of the bay – I'd reckon about a good cast away. When I turned around to notice the shore, I seen this kid standin' there watchin' us."

Suddenly his story had my complete attention.

"We figure'd we had the lake to ourselves. I gotta tell you I was mor'n a little surprised to see that kid standin' there. Looked like a boy, I'm sure. Blond hair, dirty face, wearin' them bib overalls an' a tee shirt."

Yes, I'd heard that description before. I leaned closer.

"Well, I must'a jumped a bit or said somethin' 'cause my partner turned and seen the kid too. We jus' kinda' looked at each other, an' at the kid, and the kid was just lookin' back at us.

"Finally I says, 'Hey kid, you okay? You lost? Where's your folks? Where are ya camped?' The kid just stood there starin' at us. My partner tried talkin' to him but with no more answer than I got. While he was tryin' to get the kid to talk, I'm thinkin' where'd the boy come from? There ain't no camp sites down around this end of the lake – too swampy. An' the whole time we been on the lake the past several days we hadn't seen or heard anybody else.

"Well my partner was havin' no luck gettin' the boy to answer, so I tells him 'Wait a minute, this kid is lost for sure and but good. We gotta go in an' pick him up.' So we reels in our lines, all the time talkin' to the kid on the shore who is still just standin' there starin' at us. We start paddlin' in nice and easy, and I'm tellin' the kid to just wait there and not be scared, we're comin' to help him an' everything's gonna be okay.

"But when we're about 15-20 feet from him, the kid turns an' runs up into the tag alder. Soon as we hit shore both of us took off after him, and I guess you know it was pretty tough goin'. We was bustin' through the brush an' sinkin' in over our knees in muck every other step. We called for the kid, we tried lookin' for his tracks in the muck, everything we could think to do. Only thing we did scare up was a big ol' owl that was up in a tree watchin' us stomp around in the brush. That kid sure musta been scared of us to take off into the bush like he did.

"We looked hard, my partner an' me, but after an hour or so we quit. We was tuckered out an' pretty much ate up by the bugs. Anyways, we figured we'd need some help from the rest of the gang and we went to fetch 'em. We spent the rest of the day, our whole bunch, lookin' through that area for that kid an' never found a trace or a track. We even paddl'd the whole shoreline an' checked every campsite. They was all empty, just like we figured. Not even any sign that anybody'd even been to any of 'em recently.

"Anyhow, we hung around the lake a few more days, spendin' a lot of time back in that swampy bay. But none of us ever seen that kid again. I felt real bad 'bout leavin,' but of course we had to go. Outa grub an' all, ya know. That was some years ago now, but I've never forgot…"

So, I thought to myself, people are still seeing him. I wasn't interested in hearing the rest of the stories these guys were trading anymore, so I left. The guide's story haunted me though, and I went for a long walk. He'd stirred up some old memories of my own past encounters with a young child out in the wilderness. A child about six years old, blond hair, clad in bib overalls and a tee shirt. A child I had seen several times but never met.

I recalled my first encounter years before. I was leading a group from down south on a hunting trip in the late fall. We were heading back and I was glad, since the weather was turning cold and I didn't want to get caught in the freeze up. I was trying to set a fast pace for the return trip; that's why I was first over the portage. I set my canoe in the lake with relief at the end of a good long carry. In spite of the crisp, cold air, it was a beautiful clear day. Good for traveling. I turned to shed my pack before going back up the trail to haul another load, and that's when I saw him. The kid I mean.

I was startled. There wasn't anyone close behind me on the portage, and we hadn't seen any other hunting parties, let alone any with kids along. The sun was coming through the trees behind him and I put out my hand against the light while squinting to see better. I said something like, "Hi there, where'd you come from?" The kid just stood there in those bib overalls and tee shirt looking straight at me. I turned a moment to set my pack in the canoe, and when I looked back he wasn't there. Stepping on the rocks back to more solid footing, I stared at the place where he'd been standing a moment before. I glanced around through the trees but didn't see him. It must have been one of my own group following me, I decided, and I was just confused by the sunlight. I headed back up the trail to help the others.

When I rejoined my party, I asked if anyone had been right behind me on the portage. They just laughed and said I was in too much of a hurry to keep up with. I guess I'd have noticed any of my group dressed in bib overalls and tee shirt, if they had been. Besides, none of my whiskered bunch could easily be mistaken for a kid. Still, when we'd finished the carry, I was the last canoe to push off, being somewhat reluctant to leave the portage. It felt like I was leaving that kid behind. I tried to pass it off as my imagination playing tricks on me, and didn't mention the kid to the others.

As we paddled away from the portage, I turned to look back over my shoulder against the glare of the sun light and saw him again. I turned the canoe abruptly, telling my bow man to look. Before I could explain, my bow man said, "Hey, yeah, too bad we've filled out, that'd be an easy shot." Then I noticed what he was looking at. A nice young buck bounded from the shoreline beside the portage and disappeared into the woods. "No," I said, "I mean look at…," but there was no point. There was no kid anymore. No one standing watching us.

The remainder of the trip I tried to disregard the vision, but it had seemed so real. I never told any of my party, forcing myself to believe it was the light or my imagination playing tricks on me. In fact, I never mentioned it to anyone. But it wasn't the last time I saw that kid.

The next summer I saw the child again. It had been hot and muggy and I was leading a fishing party this time. We were up on LaCroix paddling most of the length, and I'd been watching ominous clouds building in the west. When I noticed lightning in them, I knew we were in for some heavy weather, and soon. There was an island in the distance, and I knew there was a campsite on it where we could weather the storm.

We pulled hard for the island. I was well ahead of our group, wanting to get ashore first and start setting up shelter. I could see the campsite in the distance and held the bow of the canoe directly on… this young kid at the landing. At first I thought the site was occupied, but then the familiarity of those bib overalls and tee shirt sent a chill down the back of my neck in spite of the muggy air. I spun around to see if anyone else in my party had noticed the kid standing there at that campsite, but they were far behind me and concentrating on beating the storm. Turning my attention back to the campsite, I saw the child was gone again. I felt relieved, but not too surprised.

As soon as I got to the island I hauled my canoe up and stowed my gear under it. Grabbing a tent, I headed toward the first tent pad. There, on that tent pad stood the kid again.

The wind was picking up, and I could hear thunder approaching. There wasn't much time to waste. My party would soon be landing and wanting to get into shelter from the rain. But there we stood, staring at each other, me and the kid. No glare from the sun now, I could see clearly enough to make out features. Blond hair, big dark eyes. Slowly I approached the youngster, holding out the tent. Our eyes locked on each other, and looking at me very serious but without saying a word, the child slowly shook his head side to side, saying no to something.

"What?" I yelled over the growing roar of the wind in the pines overhead. "What do you mean? I've gotta get this tent set up before this storm hits." He just shook his head again, and looked off toward the approaching canoes.

"Okay, come and help me," I yelled. Big drops of rain were starting to splat around me. I threw out the tent roll and spread it out. At the same time I noticed the kid was gone again, I heard the first canoe at the landing. Soon they were up at the site and in just as big a rush to get a tent up as I was. Three guys started to set up on the first tent pad, and for some reason I yelled "no, not there." They looked at me like I was nuts, and asked "why not?" I snapped back, "just don't!"

The storm struck as I was staking the last tent. Everyone else was inside, and I got soaked before getting inside myself. A guide's lot. We huddled in our tents as the tempest raged on the other side of the canvas. The rain was tremendous, as was the thunder and lightning, but the wind was what scared me the most. We could hear the waves on the rocks and the roar in the trees around us.

Suddenly, there was a shattering crack, followed by a prolonged crashing sound which ended in a dense thud that reverberated through the island's granite core. A tree had gone down. I could hear others crashing into one another farther off, and the thumping of falling limbs hitting the ground. I yelled to the other tents to see if they were okay, but they couldn't hear me over the rain and wind. My stomach knotted while we sat in the tent waiting out the storm, knowing that tents offered us no protection at all from the trees. I weighed the idea of stepping out into the storm to see what was happening even if it meant being pelted by the cold, wind-driven rain.

Fortunately, as with most violent summer storms, this one passed quickly, before I could make the decision. As the rain let up, I opened our tent flap to see the other tents. One was still standing, the other had partially collapsed and I could hear cursing and complaining from its occupants. Turning my head, I looked over the top of our tent toward the destruction in the woods. There was the tree. A huge white pine, close to three feet in diameter at the base, had toppled. It lay directly across the tent pad where I had intended to set up the first tent. We'd have been crushed like bugs.

Later that evening before sun down, members of our party wandered around the soggy campsite assessing the damage. No one was complaining about being wet. We were all sobered by the power of the storm and the sight of that big tree lying on the tent pad. I'm sure, like me, they could still feel its impact. They all thought I must have known by some "guide's intuition" not to pitch the tent there. That somehow I knew that was where the tree would fall. For the rest of that trip, those guys never questioned a thing I told them. I knew the truth, but how could I tell them a disappearing boy told me not to tent there? Turning from the kettle on the fire I looked back at the massive log that lay on the tent pad. A red squirrel watched me from on top of the log, and then bounded into the woods.

I've seen the child other times too, but never when I've been searching for him. Every time I've seen him though, it's been in the northwestern part of the canoe country. He just seems to show up unexpectedly when he wants to. I refer to him as if he's a ghost, but that's just because it's the way he seems to be. The way he appears and disappears so quickly. I've never watched him disappear, but when he runs into the woods, it sure seems he disappears.

Once he was watching me on a portage. I was carrying my canoe when I saw him crouching on a big, mossy boulder beside the trail. I stopped, and slowly shed my canoe and pack. We just stared at each other for awhile, and I tried talking to him again. (He has never spoken to me in any of our encounters.) The boy seemed frightened of me, so I tried to reassure him. As I approached him, he slipped down behind the boulder and headed up hill through the brush and big rocky outcrops. I called for him to wait, but lost sight of him.

Scrambling up the steep slope I came to a deep crevice where a huge slab of granite had separated from a giant section of exposed bedrock. A perfect hiding place, if I were a kid. I peered into the darkness, and then stepped down into the broken rock fragments and dead leaves. With unsure footing I felt my way along the damp, cold slab of rock. In the darkness a huge, dark mass of something snuffed and grunted. I tripped and fell trying to back out and a dark mass bolted past me. I let out a yell as I went down, and caught a glimpse of a big bear's rump exiting the opening behind me. It startled me so much I completely forgot about the kid. I picked up my bruised body and limped out of the hole, brushing off leaves and moss in an effort to restore my dignity... as if anyone were watching. No kid, no bear. At that point I was glad of both.

I was most of the way across the next lake, mulling over the incident, when a thought occurred to me. I felt certain the kid went in that dark place, but a bear came out. But what could have happened inside? Could it have been that... No. Never mind. I'm not sure I want to know.

But memories of this child apparition still haunt my thoughts as I walk alone sometimes. Where did he come from? Who is he? Is he real or,... what is he?

He could be someone's lost child. Was a mother berry-picking one day and became separated from her boy? Did the child wander off on his own or was he lured off? Was he the victim of a boating accident or some other misfortune? Does he have some relationship with the animals? How does he exist in the wilderness? But perhaps he doesn't.

Some foreign countries have a name for children like this, with all sorts of fairy tales adorning what may be a shred of truth. I've heard the name "Changeling," referring to a child switched at birth for another. But there are other definitions or explanations as well. I'm not sure what to call him.

The spring after my last encounter with the boy, a friend of mine came looking for me. He said he'd been on a canoe trip with a partner, and they were having some fun running a few "good" rapids with the high water. They were about to go down an easy one that they'd run frequently in years past. Preparing to put into the fast water at a point of "commitment," he saw a kid on the river bank. The kid was shaking his head "no." He shouted over the roar of the rapids to ask why not, but the kid just shook his head. For some reason, he decided to scout this familiar rapids first.

Around the bend was a sharp drop that they would have normally gone down with no problem during spring high water. But this year, a huge slab of thick ice was jammed at an upstream angle from the rush of water. It was like a gaping maw sucking up the river and anything swept with it, and grinding it to pulp. They had thought all the ice was gone from the river, and it should have been. Yet this piece was there waiting for them. They returned to the canoe to thank the boy for the warning, but when they got back he wasn't there.

A short distance upstream, they noticed a young deer drinking from the river. When it saw them approach, it turned and went off into the willows on the bank and out of sight. There was no sign of the young boy, he was no longer around.

Or was he...?

Agamok

Some years ago a team of Canadian geologists drilling core samples in the remote tundra of the Northwest Territories, found a little wooden cask partly buried in the soil under a small cairn. It appeared to have been slowly rotting there for a very long time. Inside the cask, wrapped in some sort of oiled case, was a decaying manuscript with badly faded but still legible handwriting. One of the geologists from Quebec recognized it as a journal from the late 1700s, written in old French.

The geologists were amazed that the journal had survived both the years and the elements in a legible condition. Possibly something in the chemistry of the peat had preserved it, they thought; or maybe the long cold seasons of the far north slowed the decomposing. Whatever the case, the French-speaking geologist became engrossed in the old document. Exposed to the air, the fragile pages dried and crumbled nearly as fast as he labored his way through them. That's why no actual text remains.

Because the language was old, and the geologist was eager to read the pages before they disintegrated, he took liberties in deciphering the exact wording. It was nonetheless, a valiant effort to interpret the gist of the record, which went something like this:

The Journal of Jean Paul Barbeau
In the employ of the Northwest Company
On contract to establish and provide commerce for the Company in the territories of northwestern Canada

June 3, 1796,
Arrival at Fort near the Grand Portage

I begin this journal at the opening of my assignment, which officially started upon my present arrival at the fort near the Grand Portage, at the edge of the north-western wilderness.

We arrived at the Fort by midafternoon two days ago, and there have been celebration and festivity as is custom befitting the successful completion of the arduous journey. All are thankful for having made the voyage safely.

(A Personal Note: I am now more pleased, having arrived, that I was granted permission to travel to the fort at the Grand Portage to the frontier. Not many are anxious to make the difficult trip and face the hardships of life here, but it is a means to further one's career in this business. I left Montreal in May with a brigade in large bark canoes, traveling through the Great Lakes and across Lac Superieur. The crossing was often frightful and difficult, but our voyageurs were strong and bold. I now better understand the men called voyageurs, and how the lake and land together can leave their impression forever on one's spirit.

This wilderness is like nothing I've experienced or imagined, and mere words permit only an impoverished description, thin as the page on which they are written. This is a vast, unforgiving land of wood, water and stone. The trees themselves are impressive subjects – towering giant pines with mighty limbs and trunks of tremendous girth. Their thick roots probe the rocky bones of the earth for cold sustenance, grudgingly given. The huge lake has a moody soul of its own, at times brooding under misty shrouds, at other times tormented, raging against the rocky coast that relentlessly confines it. Here all is as God created it, untouched by anything we might call civilized. The silent, primitive landscape evokes a melancholy by its relationship to the temperamental lake. Still, there is an irresistible beauty in this land that draws one into its lonely existence, even if in brief passing. Contemplating any view along the shore, one continually wonders what might lie just beyond the next point or behind the trees.)

June 10, 1796,
The fort at the Grand Portage

The festivities accorded our arrival have subsided. I am making acquaintances and learning more about my new surroundings. The voyageurs continue to recover from their raucous celebration and the arduous trip. I have found a place to stay in a loft above the warehouse, with some other clerks. It is very crude, made of rough-hewn trees. Still, it is nice to feel secure again within roof and walls.

(Personal note: I feel compelled to mention one of the Indians, for he stands out from the others and I am curious about him. He looks, dresses and acts different from the other Indians around here, and does not seem to mix with them. They regard him as an outsider. He is a somewhat shorter and stockier fellow, with broad face, high cheek bones and a very sparse, wispy mustache. But a singular feature draws one's attention, a terrible scar from a horrendous burn. It's as though the skin melted and ran like hot wax, then cooled into a pale, undulating texture that covers the left side of his head. Little of his left ear remains, and his long, straight black hair is missing on the side of his head to just above his left eye. The scarred flesh extends down his neck apparently onto his back, where I could not see beneath his garment.

His eyes too, are somehow different from those of the other Indians. It's difficult to guess his age, though he does not appear to be very old. His was the first new face I saw as we arrived at the fort, and it shall never depart my memory. Just before I got out of the canoe I recall his studying me intensely with a look that chilled my soul. Then he was lost in the crowd that pressed to greet us.)

June 12, 1796,
The fort at the Grand Portage
Today I began the real work for which I came to this desolate place. We are doing an inventory of trade goods in preparation for a brigade which is soon leaving to supply an outpost in the northern wilderness. The fresh air and work agree with me. I feel quite strong and healthy again.

(Personal note: I've noticed the unique Indian fellow a few times, mainly from a distance. He is usually alone, and often stands on the rocks near the shore, staring off across that great body of water as if watching for some event. I have inquired about him from friends inside the fort, but they know nothing of him. They only comment on his repulsive appearance. One of the clerks told me that the Indian simply showed up on this side of the great portage a few weeks ago, and that he seems to be waiting for something or someone. I am curious about him, though for some reason he makes me feel uneasy.)

June 14, 1796,
The fort at the Grand Portage
Work continues, sometimes hard, sometimes tedious. I wonder who will use these trade goods we sort and pack into bundles. The bundles are tightly bound and very heavy, and I'm already grateful I'll not have to carry them. That is the work of a voyageur. Weather is grand and I'm enjoying this experience.

I met another interesting character today, a little fellow called Baptiste, who works in the warehouse doing menial jobs. Says he was a "hivernant" (one of the voyageurs who has traveled to the Northwest and wintered over). He dresses like a voyageur and has made many trips into that country, but walks all stooped over limping like an old man, presumably crippled by past burdens.

(Personal note: Baptiste is crude and likes to drink too much, but is in good humor all the time, laughing and singing, which makes the work easier. The clerks get him talking about the North Country and he gets carried away, telling fantastic things I won't repeat here, lest others think I too am a liar. Baptiste's fondness for drink is no doubt the inspiration for his stories, though others tell me they are true. Perhaps they are. When he talks about that country, his eyes are alight with excitement, and he seems sincere when he gets emotional because he cannot go back there anymore. His body is too old and broken from carrying the great packs on the rugged trails. He often talks about the natives, the Indians, and claims to have one as a wife who waits for him out there)

June 18, 1796,
The fort at Grand Portage

It has been raining for several days, damp, cold and foggy. Still the work goes on. I have volunteered to accompany the brigade under the leadership of Mssr. Renee Francois Sevard, leaving in early July for an outpost in the Northwest. Sevard is a Company man who has been to the wilderness before. Our departure is rather late, but I have heard that Mssr. Sevard manages to extract a full measure from his voyageurs in return for their pay.

(Personal note: I am lonely today, and miss my family in Montreal)

June 21, 1796,
The fort at Grand Portage

I am involved with making preparations for our trip to the Northwest. So far we have 23 packs of various trade goods to bring with us, and we're still packing. Sevard likes to bring much in, so he can bring the more out. We'll be carrying less food and eating light, in order to bring more goods with us.

(Personal note: I asked Baptiste about the Indian fellow with the terrible scar. Baptiste says his name is Agamok, and he comes from far to the Northwest. How he got the terrible scar Baptiste does not know for sure. But he says that some of the other Indians talk of a great fire that happened two years ago. It burned a large area in the Northwest, and reportedly wiped out an entire village of native people. If this Agamok is a survivor of the blaze, no one knows and he does not say. No one here understands his language, but Baptiste says Agamok does speak a few words of French. Why the Indian came all this way from the Northwest alone is unknown to Baptiste as well.)

June 23, 1796,
The fort at Grand Portage

Sevard is expected any day now, and after a rest, we will set out for the Northwest. I do not know who our voyageurs will be, as there are not many "hivernants" left here at the fort. Those who would go have already left for that wilderness, and the only voyageurs left here are a few canoemen from Montreal and the East who are unfamiliar with the route.

It will be mid-July by the time we set out for the Northwest, and many of the voyageurs say you can't get back here from that territory before winter. They refuse to sign-on with Sevard's brigade and risk enduring a winter in the wilderness. I suspect that they do not want to work for Sevard because of his harsh reputation.

(Personal note: I mentioned to Baptiste, the old voyageur, that I was going on a trip to the Northwest, and he became very animated. He began with advice, and then the names of old friends I should greet for him. That led to story telling, and then he started questioning me about my preparations for the winter. I told him our plan is to be back here by late fall. He grinned and suggested that starting out this late in the season, we might indeed spend the winter there, and should go prepared.

Baptiste asked who was leading the brigade. I told him it was Sevard, and all humor left his countenance. He repeated Sevard's name and spat on the ground with a curse. Baptiste said Sevard is responsible for his being so crippled – that Sevard's relentless pushing with the extra-heavy loads not only crippled him but led to the deaths of good voyageurs who were his friends. Baptiste, no longer comfortable discussing the trip, limped off with his broom to clean somewhere else. As he left, he turned with a stone-cold look and said, "Do not go, mon amie."

I must admit I am concerned, but it will take more than the words of a sentimental, rum-soaked old voyageur to keep me from this opportunity to secure my future with the company. Perhaps I'll bring an extra blanket)

June 27, 1796,
The fort at Grand Portage

The weather has been fine, with gentle warm breezes and beautiful blue skies. Preparations for our journey are nearly completed, and soon I will have a complete inventory of goods and provisions for Sevard's approval when he arrives.

June 28, 1796,
The fort at Grand Portage

Sevard and company arrived today. A similar celebration ensued as accompanied the arrival of our group. Voyageurs enjoy any excuse for festivities. The great canoes were quickly unloaded, but it seemed these new men were not acquainted with those voyageurs already at the fort. Sevard has brought a crew of inexperienced men.

Sevard would not be caught up in the celebration. Upon reaching solid footing on shore, he joined a group of Company men, and the entourage made their way toward the Great Hall inside the fort. Apparently Sevard had pressing business to discuss. I followed them closely and sat in on the meeting in the Great Hall.

We leave day after tomorrow, and I will be very busy until then. The weather, which was fine this morning, has become overcast with a chill wind out of the Northwest.

(Personal note: My first impression of Sevard came with our introduction in the Great Hall. He dresses in very fine clothes, and represents the Company well, at least by his appearance. Sevard is imposing in stature, and I'm sure the ladies would fancy him. He is all business, and exudes such a dominant air that his presence puts everyone on edge. I'm sure he is an effective commander of a brigade of voyageurs. Yet I note his dark eyes constantly shifting under their heavy brow, like some nervous thing watching from beneath a rock.

As we walked to the Great Hall, I saw Agamok among the crowd. The Indian didn't take his eyes off Sevard as we passed. My guess is that Agamok has found what, or who, he has been waiting for since he came to the fort)

July 2, 1796,
The fort at Grand Portage

Sevard has hired the canoemen from Montreal who brought him to the fort for our trip. ("Pork Eaters," Baptiste calls them, with some disdain) These men are a new crew, inexperienced as voyageurs and none have been to the Northwest before.

Sevard has brought his own man here from Montreal to be the guide of our brigade into the territories of the Northwest. His name is Bezhik Laveaux, fathered by a Frenchman to an Indian mother. He speaks both French and the local Indian tongue, a valuable asset in this business. Laveaux is rough in both speech and manner, but knows the back country routes for he has been there many times. Although he is a large man for a voyageur, I can see that he is a capable man, and valuable to Sevard. The two men seem to have an understanding

that bridges their differences, and they work well together. I am skeptical of Laveaux's character, however, though
I have just met the man.

We will be four canoes and 26 men, including Sevard and
me. The canoes are smaller with a crew of eight; one will
have just six men, and a smaller canoe will carry only
two. That will slow us down a bit. It will be difficult to
make entries in this journal while preparing for the trip,
but I will continue to write throughout the trip as my
time allows.

(Personal note: Baptiste says that inexperienced
voyageurs are the only ones who will work for Sevard,
and that they won't again after their first trip with him.
Sevard is overbearing, untrustworthy and lacks knowledge of the back country. But worse, he's demanding and
drives too hard even for a voyageur accustomed to such
toil. That's where Bezhik Laveaux comes in.

Laveaux is the enforcer of Sevard's orders while we travel, and apparently takes pleasure in carrying them out.
Since I met the man, I've found no benevolence in his
demeanor. He is a powerful bully who enjoys drinking
and fighting, and I'm told he is very good at both. This
annoys Sevard, but he either allows it or can do nothing
about it.

Baptiste further explained how on his last trip with
Sevard, Laveaux worked them so hard on portages under
such loads and frantic pace that finally Baptiste's knees
gave out and he fell, badly wrenching his back. Sevard
would have left him behind, but the other voyageurs
refused to go on without Baptiste. They carried him out,
but at a terrible price to themselves. That was Baptiste's
last trip. Baptiste implied there is something else the new
men don't know about Sevard, something that happened
in the wilderness a couple years ago. I pressed Baptiste to
tell me what it was, but he said it was just a rumor and

dared not repeat it for fear of Sevard and Laveaux.)

July 6,
(At the fort near Grand Portage)

Our parting has been delayed by a terrible event, a violent crime in this lawless land. Laveaux has been murdered, and no one knows who did it. No one saw or heard anything, but everyone knew of his violent tendencies when he was drinking. He had only been here a few days, but he had already made new enemies among the Indians and voyageurs alike. If it was an Indian, none of them will confess or testify against another. The "Pork Eaters" claim they do not know who did it, but some among them may have had motive. However, none among them or the Indians were physically capable of taking him in a fair fight. Perhaps he was taken in ambush.

He was found with his head nearly cut off, and for some strange reason his mouth stuffed full of ashes. The investigation continues, but it is doubtful we will ever know what happened.

This development will further delay the start of our trip, since Sevard is now left without a guide. There are no qualified guides left here at the fort, and experienced voyageurs are either in the back country or refuse to travel with Sevard.

Today at a Company meeting, it was suggested the Indian Agamok be our guide, since he comes from the territory to which we are going. Sevard immediately said no, adding that Agamok is an ignorant savage, and cannot be trusted. An unreasonable assumption I think, since the Indians seem to bargain with us in good faith, and often give directions if we ask. If we are to travel there, it seems Agamok is the best choice for a guide since he is from the area. A decision must be made soon. By morning we shall know what it will be, as I think the plan is to set out as soon as possible.

July 12,
(On Lac La Croix in the wilderness)

We are well under way on our journey into the Northwest Territory, and have crossed the height of land and held a small ceremony to mark the occasion. Our canoes now travel with the flow of the rivers. It has been but a few days since the big carry at the Grand Portage, which was a terrible agony. We climbed with heavy burdens over steep rocks and through swamps, but we made it. It isn't just the land and our burdens we must endure, but the continual hoards of biting insects that harass us. Still, the voyageurs managed without complaint, as they do on all portages, and they began singing as soon as they dipped their paddles on the other side. The men are a marvelous inspiration and I am too embarrassed to complain of anything in their presence.

Agamok is our guide after all. The Company men prevailed against Sevard, saying there was no one else that could do the job. The trip is too important to cancel, since the outpost we're heading to has not been visited or heard from for some time.

Though Sevard was obliged to accept Agamok as guide, I think he would rather not go at all than have him travel with us. When the Company men asked Agamok to guide our party, he looked directly at Sevard and simply replied "oui". Sevard protested, but the men in authority stood firm. Now, by all indications our guide seems to have us going the right direction, finding his way as if by instinct rather than instruments. I feel quite comfortable with his qualifications. We make steady progress, though never enough for Sevard.

(Personal note: Sevard is very angry that Agamok is our guide, and shows his resentment by being rude or ignoring him. Agamok seems unperturbed. Perhaps it is his ability to be completely at home in this wild, uncivilized environment. He seems quite comfortable, almost happy behind his solemn demeanor, in spite of Sevard's treatment of him.)

July 28,
Somewhere in the northwest wilderness

The insects are terrible, biting, no rest.

Lost a man to sickness yesterday. We have stopped to bury him as the voyageurs will not press on without doing so, (much to Sevard's apparent dismay).

We must not have much farther to travel to reach the outpost. We work as hard at maintaining our spirits as we do at travel labor, due to Sevard's constant pushing and harassing the men.

I feel obliged to report that though Sevard's leadership is commendable, if harsh, I am unimpressed by his navigational skills. He undoubtedly depended on Laveaux's ability to navigate on previous trips. This being the first trip for the men, they are unfamiliar with the route. Although I know little of navigation and nothing of this territory, from looking at our map and compass, it seems the Indian has us accurately on course. Sevard argues that this is not the route we should be taking, and disagrees with Agamok about where we are and where we should be. Agamok knows nothing of maps or compass, apparently navigating by instinct, like a migrating bird. I don't like to contradict Sevard, Yet, Agamok's directions, given in his limited French, have shown Sevard wrong many times. To the chagrin of Sevard, the men trust more in Agamok's instinct and go according to his directions. Based on my studies of the map, I tend to agree.

Yesterday we had a most difficult portage, long and wet, with rugged climbs at both ends. The middle portion went through a swamp which was nearly impossible with the heavy burdens. Sevard presses us on without rest even at the end of such a difficult carry. I don't know how the men hold up.

The weather has been good to us though; we travel mostly in sunlight, with only occasional rain. Hope we reach the outpost soon.

August 12, 1796,
Somewhere in the northwest wilderness

Today started with light rain, which turned to a fine mist. A cool breeze from the northwest picked up about midday, and it carries a faint, acrid smell, like wet ashes in a fire pit. Perhaps there has been a fire nearby.

August 13, 1796,
Somewhere in the northwest wilderness

The rain and mist have quit, but the sky remains overcast. By midday we discovered the source of the acrid smell. Crossing a portage we came to a large lake. Across that lake the land and forest are blackened by fire as far as we could see. Though some greenery is beginning to return, the sight of the burned land is disturbing, and we are headed directly into it. The scorched earth seems to have made Sevard uneasy and a bit temperamental, but we continue on our course.

Without lob trees or blaze marks, I do not know how we can find our way, but Agamok goes on, locating each portage with no apparent problem. I will not be happy until we are past this dismal, burned area.

August 15, 1796,
Somewhere in the northwest wilderness

I thought we would be past this bleak, burned out land by now, but the oppressive landscape persists. We have traveled for miles, with only charred spikes of tree trunks protruding from the blackened earth. There is hope in the fragile carpet of green vegetation struggling to return, but in the short growing season of this northern land it will take time. There is a distinct absence of wildlife, but birds are coming back and other creatures will surely follow as food sources grow back. What little food our rations allowed last night, we ate cold for lack of fuel to make a decent fire.

The endless depressing scene takes a toll on voyageurs as well. They have not been in song since we reached this burned area, and paddle mostly in silence.

Still Sevard drives the men, though he wouldn't need to now. We all want to get beyond this stretch of abandoned hell and to rest at the outpost which is our destination.

(Personal note: Agamok remains silent, as always; but I have noted Sevard has become noticeably uneasy. He glances about continuously at the passing barren shore-line, his mouth sometimes forming silent words. It is as though he's searching for something he's afraid to find. He does not bark orders as frequently now, and is more withdrawn.)

August 17, 1796,
Somewhere in the northwest wilderness

Disappointment! Can this be the right place? We reached the outpost today, but it too has burned with the world around it. Agamok has done his job and delivered us to our destination. Were we meant to come here?

There's no sign that anyone has been here since the fire. What was once a scant assembly of log buildings in a small clearing beside a river is now all charred ruin. Only burned and blackened logs lying in tumble-down disar-ray. When the forest grows back, there will be no evidence this place existed.

(Personal note: I feel compelled to relate Sevard's odd behavior upon landing at this place. His face was ashen, and he seemed unbalanced. He stumbled ashore and walked about surveying the ruins, shaking his head and mumbling to himself. I followed him into a collapsed structure through what had been a doorway. Sevard stepped over a maze of charred logs in one corner, and reeled as his eyes beheld some horror. An eerie sound that seemed to come from Sevard's heart rather than his throat hung in the air as he bolted past me toward the river. I had to see what had shaken him so severely. Peering cautiously into the dark corner, I saw a stark white human skull lying in sharp contrast to the black charcoal all around it. I retreated grimly from the ruin, past Agamok, who had watched it all from the doorway.

I have a strong feeling Sevard has been here before. I believe only Agamok and Sevard know what transpired here, and about the fire, but neither is willing to tell. Perhaps this relates to what Baptiste knew, but was afraid to tell me because of Laveaux and Sevard. I confess to apprehension about this trip ever since Baptiste's warning, and now a sense of foreboding will give me no peace. The other men feel it too I think, and hope seems to have been left behind on one of the portages)

August 19, 1796,
Near the outpost in the northwest wilderness

After the disturbing scene at the outpost, we left the site for Sevard's sake, as he seems to be emotionally disturbed by its destruction. We set up camp a day's travel downstream. Our situation is made worse as we counted on replenishing food supplies at the outpost before continuing with our trade business. Now we can do neither. The men are scattered, looking in vain I fear, for game or trying to catch fish from the river. When not in search of food, we rest, and the men work at maintaining the canoes. I have overheard grumbling, and some are saying Sevard is no longer fit to lead. Only Agamok seems unvexed by our situation, and his stoic patience irritates Sevard.

(Personal note: Sevard has not been himself since the incident at the outpost. He shuns the warmth of our fire, and as he paces about I fear there's a fever brewing in his mind. I believe his faculties have been affected, yet I don't dare discuss my concerns with him, for the least thing sets him to frightful raving. He insists we are in the wrong place, and Agamok has led us here against his orders. He claims this place is not on the map, that it doesn't even exist! Sevard also says Agamok is the cause of all our problems, and has gotten us lost. Perhaps Laveaux would have known where we are. I have learned a great deal of respect for Agamok's abilities. I cannot say if we are in the right place or not, but if we are lost, it is unlikely that the Indian is. Agamok remains an enigma to me, but to show my support and trust I gave him one of my blankets, for the nights have become chilled. He seemed unaccustomed to kindness.)

August 24, 1796,
Near the outpost somewhere in the Northwest
Sevard's frustration continues. There is talk of desertion by some of the men. Our situation does not look good here, and I feel we must move on soon.

August 26, 1796,
Near the outpost somewhere in the Northwest
This morning eight of the men quit our party and, taking a canoe, departed in a westerly direction hoping to find another outpost. Sevard threatened and cursed them, but since they had taken up arms, no one would step forward to prevent their leaving. If Laveaux were here, perhaps he could have had a different influence. Sevard misses the enforcement of his words which Laveaux provided. At least it was only eight men and one canoe, but I fear for their lives and expect we have seen the last of them.

Tomorrow we will leave, continuing downstream, an easterly direction, toward Hudson Bay. We must make our way out of this desolate, abandoned place. I hope we find fresh, green living earth again soon, for this is more oppressive than my soul can much longer bear. We must find food.

(Personal note: Sevard continues to place the blame for our predicament on Agamok, and accuses him in the midst of the men, of a multitude of ludicrous things. He even accused him of stealing food. He may physically attack Agamok one day, I fear. Sevard has assigned someone to watch the Indian, a boring task since he does little but observe us in silence.)

August 27,
On the river somewhere in the Northwest

We have left the bulk of our trade goods in the ruins of the outpost, and set out down the river. It is good to be under way again. Overcast today, and though the northerly breeze is light, it has none of the feel of summer in it.

There seems to be a better feeling among the men today, now that we are traveling again. Hopefully we make our way toward more hospitable shelter with kind hosts. Considering our situation, it's easy to forget that this land is Agamok's home, and only he seems to know where we are and where we are going. That troubles Sevard a great deal, but the rest of us are in better spirits today, taking a course we hope will bring us out of this scarred land.

September 1, 1796,
On a river somewhere in the Northwest

Today a cold and dismal rain began falling, befitting our mood as we continue down the river. The voyageurs are not the cheerful crew we started with, singing as they paddled. That seems so long ago now, as if a year of seasons has passed in a number of weeks. A couple of the men do not get along, and argue frequently. One threatened the other with his knife last night, and I was fortunate to be able to bring them to their senses. What is to become of us?

(Personal note: Sevard continues brooding, and concentrates on fantasizing about Agamok, while ignoring the rest of us. He stays away from the fire, and even avoids looking at it. He has become more temperamental, consumed by animosity toward the Indian. It is now Sevard's only focus. Agamok remains cautiously distant, as though he is waiting)

September 3, 1796,
On a river somewhere in the Northwest

Snow flurries in the air this morning. Nothing much, and it is sunny now but the air is quite cool. We make good time on the river, as the current has picked up considerably. Two of the men are sick, but we travel on.

On the good side, we have left the burned area behind us, but there is little to forage this time of year, and we have not seen any game to speak of.

September 4, 1796,
On a river in the Northwest

Catastrophe! One of the many rapids we have encountered has dealt us a severe blow which cost us dearly. Our lead canoe, the one that carries Sevard, was midway through a frightful torrent when the craft failed to negotiate a turn and was dashed against a massive jagged rock. The canoe broke in two, spilling its occupants and cargo into the foam.

One of the voyageurs was caught between the canoe and the rock and was crushed by force of the water. Two more men rode the free half of the canoe over a drop and were sucked down in an undertow and drowned. A fourth man's body was found a mile downstream as we searched for salvageable supplies.

It was a miracle that anyone survived, but especially Sevard. His life was spared by the heroism of Agamok. I witnessed it, or I would not believe it. The Indian brought the semi-conscious Sevard to the safety of the bank about 100 yards downstream, just before he would have entered another cataract.

Our canoe capsized and we lost some supplies, but nothing else. Fortunately, my journal and our business papers stayed dry, bound in the oiled leather case which I carry over my shoulder. The men are making repairs on our canoe as I write this, and we are drying things by fires and in the brisk sunlit air.

An accounting of our losses: four lives, one canoe, maps and navigational aids, food, four muskets and gunpowder, blankets, tools and a few trade goods and miscellaneous articles. The consequences of this loss are grave indeed. We will wait here a day to honor our dead and try to recover some of our losses.

September 8, 1796,
Along a river in the wilderness

There has been more talk of desertion among some of the men. They are growing more discouraged and the disaster at the last rapids has been hard on us all. Sevard makes threats, but without Laveaux, all that keeps the men here is that none of them know where we are or where to go. At least we are together and perhaps there is comfort in that.

I am just a clerk, but I need to decide if it is in the Company's interest that I take charge of what's left of our brigade, since Sevard no longer seems competent.

(Personal note: Last night Sevard attacked Agamok in a violent rage, claiming he was responsible for the disaster at the rapids and all else that has gone wrong. This time he beat him with a stick. Agamok did not resist, and I feared Sevard would kill him, so I intervened. I thought Sevard would start beating me, but he stopped and stared at me a moment, then turned and walked off. The look in his eyes was that of a truly tormented soul. Very frightening.

I am beginning to believe Sevard is linked to the terrible fire, and Agamok knows it. I am sure this is Agamok's homeland, but we have seen none of his people. I fear they may have perished in the holocaust, and perhaps Agamok has been left alone...

We are now in dire circumstances, with Sevard a liability.

October 2, 1796,
On a large lake somewhere in the wilderness

The river we were on has emptied into a large lake, and we have made camp on an island. We are lost without the map and compass, and must search the lake for the outlet of the river before we can continue. Some men have gone to hunt again, but usually all they can find are a few ptarmigan or rabbits.

(Personal note: Weather is getting colder, and some of the men are taken ill, weak from exhaustion and lack of food. I have not been well myself. Last night Agamok returned the blanket I gave to him. A kindness that tells me his heart is not cold.

Sevard's mental state is completely irrational, and I have taken charge of the brigade. Winter is approaching and I would like to press on, but in our present physical state we are unable to do so. The possibility of canoe travel will soon be lost when ice sets in.

Sevard alternates between states of total unresponsiveness and bouts of incoherent rambling. In one of his better moments, Sevard told me he believes Agamok is some sort of demon. I thought he was our only hope, but now I am not so sure.)

October 17, 1796,
Final entry

If anyone finds this record, do not search for us. Our fate is certain now, and our remains will be long gone by the time this is read. I regret that I cannot send word to my family in Montreal that I won't be coming back. None of us will. Snow is falling as I write this, and it gathers like a white balm covering both scorched and green earth with its soothing peace.

I awakened early today, and in the first dim light of morning watched the Indian Agamok – silent as a shadow – set the small canoe in the water. He looked back towards Sevard's tent a moment, then got in the canoe and paddled off without a sound. He has gone to be with his people. I could have tried to stop him but I did not. I could have awakened the others, but I did not. As he faded in the misty distance, I turned so I would not see which way he went.

Letting Go

Rivers are a gathering of water, small streams seeking and joining each other, growing larger and stronger in their journey to the sea, for that is the nature of rivers.

But not every river.

It's the middle of the night, no particular hour. A slow, steady, spring drizzle hangs in the air. Amid a cluster of small homes in an aging residential area, a garage door opens to release an early model station wagon. Fatigued and rusting beneath the paint, the faithful old family chariot rumbles quietly down the driveway.

After negotiating a few neighborhood turns, the car is on a local thoroughfare, heading for the edge of town. It makes a rolling pause under a flashing red traffic signal that glares crimson off the shiny wet pavement. In vain, the gaudy light tries to call attention to the lone vehicle on the vacant street. The station wagon turns onto a deserted northbound highway and gradually accelerates to a sensible highway speed. The radio is off. The only sounds above the hum of the engine are tires slapping pavement seams, and the rhythm of the windshield wipers.

The driver is a woman of late middle-age, with close-cropped hair dyed to hide the gray, and telltale stress lines etched in her face. Pale green dashboard light glistens off a single, silent tear that tracks her cheek as she drives through her thoughts. In the back is a small travel bag. On the seat beside her, next to her purse, is an old packet of letter-folded papers, wrapped in a thick rubber band.

It isn't the first time she's started this trip, but the other times there was always something that called her back. Always it was something someone else needed, some reason she had to stay. At any of those times it might have been memories, might have been hope, maybe a sense of responsibility. At another time it would have been a mother's commitments to her children, her home, her marriage, that would have made her turn back. Those things were all gone now. Even after the reasons she recognized were all gone, something had held her back. Perhaps it was some written record, evidence of what had once been, some piece of a memory. Whatever unnamed thing it was, it had to do with that packet of papers. Whatever it was, it had always made her come back.

She'd been through the papers often enough to know what they said, there was no need to go through them again. Besides, they were from long ago, none of it mattered anymore. They were just useless old papers, but this time they were with her in the car.

On any other night, the late hour and the steady rhythm of the road might have lulled her to sleep, but not this time. She was wide awake, as she had been on many other sleepless nights. The continuous view of the car's hood swallowing up the highway might mesmerize some lone, late night drivers. For her, the highway rolled like a reel of film through a projector, bringing events of her life in and out of focus like an old family movie.

She recalled her childhood in a northern town, old school friends, picnics and holidays, family activities and vacation trips to the North Shore. Then there was high school, the awkward teen years, the trauma of relocation and separation from friends. Before she could make new ones, she was off to college, and then on to the challenge of a new job where she had met her husband.

For well over half her lifetime, she had been totally devoted to him, his career, their children and their home. It had been over for a number of years, and he was long gone now. Their children were grown and on their own, and she hadn't lived in that house for years. Now grandchildren were on the way. Memories of raising her family kept surfacing – both the bitter and the sweet – as wet highway now flowed beneath her like a river.

Throughout it all, she had been strong. She had once read Nietzsche's words: "What does not destroy us makes us stronger." If it were true, she should be strong indeed. She had not felt strong, but she did not feel bitter either. She had made up her mind from the beginning not to be bitter, and believed she was, at least, successful in that. She had been determined to establish her independence after he was gone, and in the process assert herself as a new individual.

Somehow though, there remained a tie, some remnant of the relationship. There was nothing left of him – of his –in her home anymore, but a connection of sorts remained. No, it wasn't him, but something else she could not let go of. It held some part of her to what she had once been, and prevented her from moving on in her life. It was bound somehow in the packet of papers beside her.

The mist had quit falling, and the slick river of highway now dropped, cascading through low clouds into the predawn lights of Duluth. The lights brought her out of her thoughts, refocusing her attention on driving, and that the fuel indicator now showed the tank was near empty. In the city, she pulled up to the self-service island of the first convenience store she found. While the tank filled, she opened the hood and found the oil to be low. She went inside to pick up a quart of 10W30 and pay for the gas.

There were no other patrons at that hour of the night, only a lone attendant at the counter who seemed too engrossed in some other matter to give her any attention.

She picked out a can of oil and went to the counter to pay. As she approached, she saw he was studying several maps of the northeastern Minnesota lake country, and writing in a spiral-bound notebook. He didn't notice as she quietly approached the counter, and she waited patiently for him to finish writing.

He was about six feet tall and lean, with graying hair pulled back and in a pony tail. She noted the frayed cuffs of his thermal underwear protruding from the rolled-up sleeves of an old flannel shirt. At the same time, she had an intuitive feeling about the man, and moved closer along the counter for a better look.

She could see he wore wire-rimmed glasses, and had a mustache that matched his gray hair. He seemed about her age, but she still couldn't see his face clearly.

After waiting for him to notice her, she got his attention by asking if he was planning a canoe trip.

He looked up, offering an apology and a more sociable demeanor for someone working a lonely night shift. He said that he was in fact looking for a canoe route, and started to ring up her gas and oil.

"Jerry?" she said. "Jerry Siverson?"

"Yeah...?" he answered, looking more deeply into her face. "Who're you? Do I know you?"

"Well, you ought to," she replied, "from high school."

"Oh, fer cryin' out... Ann! Ann Palovich!" he announced loudly to the otherwise unoccupied store. "It's been what...? Over 30 years for sure."

They extended hands, then laughed at the formality and stretched to embrace over the counter.

"Jeez, I can't believe I didn't recognize you," he said, "but how did you recognize me?"

"Well, I know I've put on a few pounds," Ann admitted, "but it's not like you haven't changed. I guess something just seemed familiar about you. By the way, my name hasn't been Palovich for a long time now."

"Yeah, I'd heard you were married. How's the family?" he asked, drawing a cup of coffee from the machine and handing it to her.

"Oh, they're all gone now, I ah… I guess I'm on my own right now."

Sensing an uneasy subject, he quickly changed it.

"So what brings you back to town?" he asked in a cheery, casual tone.

"I guess I don't know for sure, but it's sure good to see an old friend," she said, and took a sip of the coffee, "What have you been up to?"

"Well," he started, "right now I'm the night manager of this place, but it's taken me a long time to get here. I'm afraid my life took a few bad turns after high school.

"Oh, I heard you went to Viet Nam. Is that what you mean?" she asked.

"Yeah. I saw a lot of combat while I was there, did a lot of things that bothered me more than I thought they would. Let's just say I did a lot of things that I'm not proud of, things I don't tell people about. In a wartime situation, you don't think about what you're doing – that comes later. Later it was about all I could think of. Anyway, the army saw fit to give me some medals for what I had done, but even years later I couldn't feel good about it. Kept having bad dreams, you know, like the veterans with problems that you hear about on TV. I started drinking, even tried drugs for awhile, but nothing I did helped me sleep any better. I guess I really made a mess of my life, and it cost me my marriage. Eventually I went through treatment and cleaned up my act, but the dreams remained. I couldn't seem to let go. I tried therapy for awhile, but it didn't give me any peace either. When I thought I would just have to have to live the rest of my life like that, I even thought about suicide. It was not a good time in my life.

"Good Lord, I had no idea you'd been through all that," she said, "what did you do?"

"Well, now I think I've put things back together. I've got a good job working here and spend as much of my free time as I can on the water and in the woods. I like the peace and quiet," he added.

"I wish I could find that in my life," she said half to herself. "How did you manage to turn things around?"

"Remember when you came in here Ann, you asked if I was planning a canoe trip?" he said, "That's what I do for fun. But let me tell you why.

"I used to paddle lakes in the canoe country, but I started paddling rivers," he continued. "Rivers are all different in their character, having been influenced by – as well as influencing – the land they pass through, always changing with their circumstances. Sometimes the water runs deep and slow with subtle undercurrents. Other times it's rushing over falls or rapids. You never know what's around the next bend…"

"Sort of like a metaphor for life itself," she offered.

"Exactly," he responded. "That's what I like about paddling rivers. It's like life. And rivers come together, as do people's lives…" he started to go on but she interrupted.

"But that's not quite true," she said, "Unlike rivers, people don't always stay together. Sometimes instead of flowing together, people's lives split apart and they go their separate ways."

"Well, usually, but not all rivers," he replied. "I found one up the shore that splits apart."

"This one is special to me. Let me tell you why," he said. "I'd heard about this river, and once on a trip up the shore I followed it upstream about a mile and a half, two miles inland from the Lake to where it splits. I wasn't really prepared the first time I saw it.

"Like all rivers along the North Shore, this one has numerous rapids and waterfalls. But this one waterfall is split at the top by a big rock in the middle of the stream. Half of the river goes over a 50 foot drop and continues down to Lake Superior. The other half of the river drops down into a 12 to 15 foot diameter hole in the rock, and disappears into the earth – forever."

"Forever?" she asked skeptically, "You mean it never comes out anywhere? How do you know that?"

"Because some years back the Forest Service tried to find out where it went," he explained. "They put some marker dye in the water going down the hole, and had lookouts stationed at the mouths of rivers up and down the shore, and along other streams and lakes. The dye never showed up anywhere. Another time they lowered some electronic sounding equipment down the hole to determine its depth, but couldn't. Too many false echoes off the rock, I guess.

"Anyway, the point is, that waterfall had a very important influence in my life," he told her.

"How? What do you mean?" she asked.

"One day, a couple months after I'd first seen the water going down that bottomless hole in the earth, it occurred to me what I had to do. I had to go back there. I hiked back to the falls, and jumped from boulder to boulder until I was out on the rock in midstream above the waterfall. I remember how scary it was looking into that thundering hole as it swallowed up half the river. I had brought my war medals with me. I thought about the war, about what the medals represented, the memories I couldn't seem to shake. Then I threw them all down that hole. As soon as I did it, I felt better. Oh, everything didn't change all at once of course, but I felt a peace come over me. I hadn't known peace like that since before my time in Viet Nam. Something happened there at that falls, and I knew I was going to be OK.

"That night I slept peacefully, and I have ever since. It might not be what other guys would have done, but for me it was a healing thing to do. I guess it was a way to let go of some things that were holding me back. Things that were doing me more harm than any good that might have come from those medals.

"That's another reason why I like rivers, why I find them so interesting. And that's it. That's my story. "

"I had no idea," she said, "I'm glad you're doing better now though." Very interesting, she thought to herself.

A bell rang as another customer came through the door and interrupted their conversation.

"But I'd better be going now, it's been great talking with you. Let's keep in touch. I hope you find a good river. Goodnight."

"Yeah, thanks," he said, then looking into her eyes a moment he added "I hope you find one too. Good night," he responded as she headed out the door.

She backed out the door and headed for her car. She had listened to his story, especially the part about letting those medals go down that great hole. As she pulled out of the gas station, her mind whirled with all sorts of thoughts, mostly involving rivers, rushing water, and a great dark hole.

She stopped at an all-night fast-food restaurant and picked up a cup of coffee and a breakfast sandwich. She ate the sandwich and sipped the coffee as that one thought circulated, as though caught in an eddy of her mind, and it continued once she was back in her car again. Soon, whether by conscious choice or not, she was cruising the highway along the north shore of Lake Superior, as soft gray dawn forced its way through the heavy overcast. She wasn't sure where it was, but she knew where she needed to go.

It took several hours, and she stopped to ask questions or get directions a few times. Sometimes, people didn't know what she was talking about when she inquired about a waterfall that went down a hole in the rock, but she was persistent. As she got farther up the Shore, she found people who had heard of the falls, or at least knew what she was talking about. Eventually, she found someone who knew where it was and told her how to find it. She continued on, now with a real mission in mind for the first time since setting out from home. She now felt almost drawn to this place.

By late morning she parked the station wagon on an apron off the highway. Taking her purse, she stuffed the packet of papers inside, and started hiking up a trail that followed the wild river's course.

Still running high with late spring run-off, the river tumbled noisily between dark granite banks over a boulder-strewn bed. The rough and rocky trail continued for a quarter of a mile or so, then rose in a steady climb through the budding birches and freshening pines. Faithfully following the river's course, the trail offered occasional vistas of the rushing water below. She hiked past several drops, and a couple waterfalls, but nothing that fit the description Jerry had given her. She began to wonder if this was the right river. Finally, after a long stretch of steady climbing beside a waterfall she could hear but not see, she stepped out onto a rocky ledge high above the river.

Clutching her purse, she crept closer to the edge of the ledge for a better look, and peered into clouds of mist rising from the thundering falls below and the wild, raw beauty of the scene. The river indeed was split by a natural wedge of bedrock that jutted upstream from the top of the falls. From there, half of the river fell some 50 feet to where it continued its flow beside the path she'd followed, and on to the Great Lake.

The other half of the river poured itself hell-bent into oblivion down a dark hole in the solid rock. It was true, Jerry was right about the river. She needed to be closer to the falls, and the trail continued on upriver, but a spur led off down a steep climb over rocks and roots to the top of the falls.

At the edge of the river she could feel the mist on her face, and though the falls were very close, the roar seemed deceptively distant because it came from below. The bedrock island that split the falls was midstream before her, but she needed a way to get out onto it. Just a short distance upstream was a series of boulders that – with some courage and a couple good jumps – could provide the route. Good thing she'd worn sneakers. Making sure her purse was tightly closed, she swung it onto her back and lifted the strap over her head, cross-body style for security. After closing her eyes for a brief prayer, she made her way across the boulders, and with a final leap landed on the bedrock island.

Pleased with her courage, she looked downstream toward the top of the falls, and cautiously approached the side that went into the hole. As she got closer, the sound from

the opening seemed unnatural and unnerving. The res-
onating roar trapped inside the megaphone of rock was
more like a deep infernal moan.

Standing before the abyss, she began to comprehend the
nature of all it represented. She realized there was no exit
from the unknown void, no certain depth. Venturing as
close as she dared to the cavernous opening, she looked
down into the darkness and immediately felt a sense of
pity even for the water that hurled itself into the depths.
The scene gave her the distinct impression of lost hope,
and she shuddered to imagine any living thing being
flushed down there. Whatever went down that great hole
would never live, would never see the light of day again
or feel the warmth of the sun, would never again breathe
fresh air. Even in death, anything down that hole would
not be part of the natural cycle of life and death here on
the sunlit surface. To go down the abyss would not just be
ceasing to exist, but ceasing to have ever existed. As she
looked into the moaning darkness of the great maw she
could feel its misty breath on her face, could feel its sucking, invisible pull, like one standing on the brink of a
precipice. She turned away from its spell before losing
her balance, and took a couple careful steps backward.

The time had come. She opened her purse and took out
the packet of papers and held them in both hands. For a
moment, everything that the papers had represented – a
part of her life that was her pain, her sadness, her weakness, her growth, her strength – replayed itself in her
mind. There were old memories of him and things that
had happened in another lifetime. Things that could
have been, but weren't; should not have been but were.
All of the things that for one reason or another had held
her back. Now was the time to let them go.

Looking into the abyss with its mad cataract of water, she

prepared to hurl the packet of papers into oblivion. Arm cocked, she was ready to make the throw, then paused. She could not do it. She could not condemn what had happened to her – for better or for worse – to such a fate. The ordeals that had caused her to suffer over the years were as much a part of her life as were the moments that had brought her joy. These things had made her life what it was, were responsible for shaping the person she'd become. She had grown in character and was stronger for having weathered the floods and droughts in her life. They were the events of her life after all, flowing turbulently or placidly to some final destination. Perhaps things that come from the abyss were meant for the abyss, but not the experiences and relationships that constituted and shaped her life.

She turned, and let the packet go into the river on the other side. Immediately caught by the current, the papers went over the falls and down to the river below where they became unbound. She watched them disperse, bobbing on the surface as they continued downstream with the current, and out of sight. Long-awaited sunlight beamed through the parting veil of clouds and danced on the river as the papers floated away. For the first time in many years she felt bathed in a deep sense of peace.